DOCTOR G(

The Power of Cobalus

Written by

JACK WEBB

Illustrated by

GARY STOCKER

Copyright © 2021 Jack Webb

All rights reserved.

ISBN: 9798737292966

DOCTOR GOBLINS!

The Power of Cobalus

	Foreword and Notes	vii
	Acknowledgements	ix
1	Cobalus, The Shadow	1
2	Fleeing	14
3	Flying	27
4	Decisions, Decisions!	40
5	The Goblin Who Vanished	52
6	Shaston	66
7	Looking for Loca	79
8	The Wand of Ypsilon Thrubb	91
9	Molly	103
10	The Bogeyman	114
11	The Pond of Reflection	129
	About This Book	142

BY THE SAME AUTHOR

Cedric's Busy Week

The Adventures of Cedric the Spider (2018)

Cedric's Holiday

The Further Adventures of Cedric the Spider (2019)

Cedric's Christmas

The Festive Adventures of Cedric the Spider (2020)

FOREWORD

Readers of the adventures of Cedric the Spider and his two friends, Belinda and Bertie Brush, will already be acquainted with the March Meadow residence of the Evershed family in the small Suffolk village of Wicksham Parva. The house backs on to fields leading to Tanglewood, the home of the doctor goblins, Locum and Ten Ends, as well as being a regular haunt of Cedric, Bertie and Belinda who would frequently creep out through the cat flap on yet another nocturnal adventure.

But in this book we shall leave Cedric and his friends behind to tell the interwoven tales of the two doctor goblins, one venturing out from the leafy security of Tanglewood in the present day, the other on his youthful journey to Tanglewood some forty years earlier.

NOTES

Doctor Goblins

1. Cobalus, The Shadow – spirit of the Doctor Goblins. The term Cobalus is also used to describe the energy force (the Power of Cobalus) which all doctor goblins possess.
2. Cobalus Professor – distinguished pedagogue
3. Principal Doctor Goblin – Senior Principality Medical Officer
4. Assistant Principal Doctor Goblin
5. Apprentice Doctor Goblin (The Chosen Few)
6. Doctor Goblin – long-eared species of goblin with the Power of Cobalus

   Also: Cobalt – Ghost Eagle, the messenger of Cobalus

The bygone tale of Locum's apprenticeship can be recognised by a change in font (from Calibri to Times New Roman) and with the font colour in sepia.

ACKNOWLEDGEMENTS

Profound thanks go to:

My friends and family members for allowing me to encrypt their names as characters in my fictional tales.

My multi-talented illustrator Gary, who so brilliantly brings these stories to life and informs the process of publication; also, his colour consultants, daughters Lilia and Alyssa.

My children Edmund and Emily, who prompted me to set in writing the bedtime stories I had dreamt up when they were young and who added valued critical suggestions to the editing process; also my granddaughter Chloe whose advice on format and style stemmed from the apposite viewpoint of a ten-year-old.

Finally, I am constantly indebted to my dear wife Brenda who patiently listens to the day's output and lives the unfolding stories with me.

DOCTOR GOBLINS!

CHAPTER 1

COBALUS, THE SHADOW

Locum's little goblin home lay hidden beneath an earthy, fern-covered hump in the far reaches of Tanglewood Deep. Despite its remoteness, this secluded glade was frequently visited by nature's little pilgrims, often travelling great distances across eastern England to seek a cure for their various ailments and maladies. Rabbits with fox bites, hares wounded by shotgun pellets, owls with watery eyes, digging moles with sore feet, grass snakes with rheumatism, all would come to see Principal Doctor Goblin Locum, with his profound knowledge of herbal remedies, natural ointments and creams, potions made from berries and, on rare, but often memorable occasions, his astonishing ability to employ the power of Cobalus, bringing a breath of spirit back to the lifeless.

Despite his size, just about the height of a milk bottle, his strange, some would say ugly appearance and his brusque couch-side manner, he was, nevertheless, a truly dedicated and wonderful physician who hated to see any of God's creatures in pain. His special gifts were all the more effective because he always used them for the benefit of others. In contrast, his neighbour Ten Ends was a vastly different character altogether. Impetuous, like many youngsters in their early twenties, he was a melting pot of mischief and benevolence, meanness and compassion, cruelty and kindness, a troublemaker and yet, a healer. Though sorely tested, Locum still believed that in an acute crisis Ten Ends would ultimately choose the virtuous path. Others had their doubts.

On a clear, moonlit Spring night, Ten Ends wandered out of Tanglewood towards the nearby village of Wicksham Parva. He was looking for something to sweep away his boredom and fill the hours of darkness with adventure and excitement. He considered that his life, of late, had been far too dull. Ideally, he wanted an object which, using his talents as a doctor goblin, he could spark into life.

Because of his ambivalent nature, Ten Ends' use of the life-giving power of Cobalus was unpredictable. Back in the depths of time, Cobalus, The Shadow, had gifted the power to his ancient doctor goblin ancestors. It had been passed from generation to generation for the benefit of earth's creatures rather than for mischief, trickery and pranks. When Ten Ends was being helpful and kind, his use of the

Cobalus power tended to be more successful, but when his behaviour was wayward, it became less so. Unfortunately, Ten Ends did not always think whether his actions were good or bad, they were inclined to be mere whims. He could deploy Cobalus in good faith and it would, at times, be successful, though neither he nor anyone else could be certain of the outcome.

On the edge of the village, a farm track led to an old barn in which an assortment of farm equipment was stored. Ten Ends managed to squeeze under the barn door, briefly allowing his eyes to grow accustomed to the shadowy darkness within, then looked around to select a suitable machine for experiment.

Could he, perhaps, breathe life into a combine harvester? That would be great fun, though difficult and also potentially dangerous. He needed to find something that could do no harm, perhaps even do some good, thereby making the power of Cobalus far more effective.

He stood for a while, gazing round and weighing up his options. *"A tractor? Again, a bit big for starters. Perhaps something smaller and easier to control. Ah! A lawnmower! I could help the villagers tidy up their gardens. They would be so pleased to wake up in the morning and find that their grass had been cut. But what about the engine noise? No problem. If Cobalus works, the mower will come to life and I could ask it, politely of course, to run in silent mode. Perfect, a lawnmower it shall be!"*

The machine Ten Ends eventually happened upon had been described by Farmer Jay as somewhat tired and unreliable. It had been sitting in the barn all winter waiting for a service and clean up. Its once bright green paint had for the most part been replaced by grime and rust, but none of this deterred Ten Ends. As the Cobalus ritual required, he stared down at its cutting blades, focussed his eyes with penetrating intensity and, breathing heavily on the old mower, began to rub his pointed ears with his tiny goblin fingers … and … nothing happened.

He had to clear his head and forget his misgivings. *"What if it goes wrong and I end up in trouble again? I'd have to face Wye's Owl and Locum and they wouldn't be best pleased. What if the mower turns on me and I end up on a compost heap? No. Empty your head and dismiss such thoughts. Concentrate, Ten Ends, concentrate!"*

Once again, the little goblin began to invoke the power of Cobalus. After a moment or two, with his attention firmly fixed on the old contraption, he suddenly noticed a slight rotation of the drum mower blades. As the revolutions increased, other parts of the engine and frame, those which were normally bolted and rigid, began to stir and flex. Before long, the whole mower had come to life and, with a stretch and a shake, it began to move forward.

"Stop!" shouted Ten Ends. "Wait for my instructions. Let me climb aboard."

"And 'oo are you to give me orders?" The deep booming voice appeared to emanate from the depths of the grass box. The mower had paused and was staring at Ten Ends with two small eyes that had appeared on the ends of its handlebars which, as if made of rubber, were able to twist and turn in order to peer in any direction.

Ten Ends quickly introduced himself as a doctor goblin from Tanglewood, a friend of Locum and Wye's Owl.

"And you? Do you have a name?"

The mower thought for a moment. "As Oi remember Oi were built in a factory in Ipswich. Oi think it were called 'andsomes. So you can call me Handsome if you loike."

"Hardly appropriate," Ten Ends thought but kept his opinions to himself. *"And now for the real test ..."*

"If you don't mind, Handsome, I'd like to climb up and take you out for a spin. What do you say?"

"Oi sez, foine, young sir! Anything is better than sitting in this draughty ol' shed all day and night, bored out of me cylinders. Jump aboard!"

"Just one thing before we set off. We mustn't make any noise or we'll be heard. Can you run silently?"

"Oi can now," Handsome's eyes lit up. "All of a sudden Oi seem to have complete control of my engine, switches and levers. Me mind's me own since you happened by. Let's be off, little goblin!"

With that, the intrepid pair crashed through the rotten timbers of the old barn door leaving it hanging from its hinges, then set off merrily towards the village green.

What they did not know, however, was that all these goings on had been observed by a sleepy old barn owl peering down from the rafters. Brenda Hoot realised that mischief was afoot and felt it her duty to report to Wye's Owl and Locum, although she thought, mistakenly, that it could wait until the following morning.

By the time Ten Ends and Handsome had reached the village green, it had become quite apparent that the former had little, if any, control over the latter. Handsome was relishing his newly found independence while Ten Ends was clinging on for dear life, with occasional despairing and futile shouts of "Left a bit … slow down … NOT THERE … STOP!!!"

It also transpired that Handsome had, throughout his life, grown tired of mowing in neat, straight lines and had always wondered why he was only ever allowed to cut grass, grass mind you – green and boring! This was the perfect opportunity to express himself, to release his artistic consciousness and demonstrate his mowing prowess. Lowering his blades, he proceeded to reduce beautifully groomed garden lawns to a stripped shaving of mud, he cut circles and patterns on the village green cricket pitch, he hacked down the pretty spring flowers in the memorial gardens and emptied the contents of his grass box at regular intervals all along the high street.

As dawn approached Ten Ends, in a state of disbelief and horror, grew evermore dejected and powerless. All his requests and commands were totally ignored by the frenzied mower. Yet, when the day of reckoning finally arrived, he knew full well on whose shoulders the blame would fall. He shuddered to think of the punishments that would be meted out to him by Wye's Owl and Locum, the senior figures in the Tanglewood law council. But what scared Ten Ends even more was the possibility of being spotted by a human in daylight.

Cobalus, The Shadow, monitored all goblin activity, and doctor goblins were no exception. If they were spotted by a human after sunrise, they would immediately be petrified forever as a frozen garden gnome. Countryfolk would occasionally come across one and take it home as a rockery ornament. Finders keepers!

Frightened to face the dressing-down which would undoubtedly await him in Tanglewood, Ten Ends decided to leave Wicksham Parva and lie low somewhere distant for a day or so. While Handsome was still continuing to wreak havoc on the village recreation ground, he took a flying leap off the wayward mower, tumbled on to the soft turf and scurried away as fast as he could to the shelter of the nearby cricket pavilion, just seconds before three watchful observers happened to fly across the green.

At first light, Brenda Hoot had finally ventured over to Tanglewood and alerted Wye's Owl to the events in Farmer Jay's barn. Fully aware of Ten Ends' potential for mischief, they had picked up Doctor Locum from Tanglewood Deep and, for the past hour or two, had been scouring the village, aghast at the widespread damage that they could see beneath them. Eventually they spotted Handsome the lawnmower, who had, incidentally, just knocked over the local football team's goalposts. Unfortunately, Ten Ends did not appear to be with him or, for that matter, anywhere else nearby.

Flying down to the green, the two owls watched as Locum sought to bring the mower under control. The power of Cobalus was deep-seated in this remarkable little doctor goblin and Handsome was rapidly rendered lifeless and parked up next to a mound of cut grass. Later that morning, the matter would be reported to the police by some public-spirited villager, Farmer Jay would take Handsome back to the barn on his tractor and trailer, while a number of local ne'er-do-wells would be rounded up for questioning!

*****

The sun rose and the streets of Wicksham Parva stirred gently into life. Ten Ends realised that the risk of being spotted grew greater as the milkman, postwoman and farm labourers set about their daily round. He had to leave the village where he was most likely to be seen and recognised by local birds, beasts and insects, and find a hiding place devoid of human activity. His little legs would not permit fast travel, yet the risk of staying in Wicksham Parva was far too great. He needed transport. His experience with Handsome the mower had taught him that using Cobalus on vehicles was extremely risky. He dreaded to think where he might end up on board a rampant milk float with a mind of its own.

At that point, an idea struck him. On the pavement alongside the village green stood a shiny red post box. Ten Ends knew that people had to post their letters by late afternoon. At 4 o'clock a red van would arrive to collect the day's mail and transport it in a sack to the regional sorting office in the town of Markstow, some seven miles away. No animals there would recognise him. He could hide up in town until the heat was off and the devastation wreaked by Handsome the lawnmower was forgotten. Locum and Wye's Owl, given time, would be relieved that he was safe, and any punishment would be light. Peering round the pavilion picket fence, he waited until the coast was clear, dashed across the green, scampered up the side of the postbox and squeezed through the mail slot, safely out of sight.

During the day, numerous letters and small parcels rained down on Ten Ends' hat, one of which, being quite heavy, gave the little goblin a mild headache, no more, you may say, than he deserved. The postbox itself was lined with a fitted plastic sack, complete with string ties. Right on time at 4 o'clock, the mail was removed by Penny Black, the postwoman, who secured the ties and fitted an empty bag in readiness for the next day's mail. Penny loaded the hefty sack filled with letters, small packages and, unknown to her, Ten Ends the doctor goblin, into her van, and set off for the sorting office in Markstow.

Late that afternoon, after she had finished making collections from a number of other postboxes in the mid-Suffolk area and was finally back at the depot, Penny, with tired, aching limbs, unloaded the bags on to barrows which were then towed indoors for sorting by her friend Drew Fowler.

"Long day, Penny?"

"What's new, Drew! Still, time to go home at last, make m'self a cuppa and put m' feet up."

"Good for you. My day, or should I say night, is only just beginning!"

The work of the sorting office was undertaken by the night shift. The sacks of mail and parcels collected from village post offices and boxes were emptied and their contents sorted by post code. Letters were scanned by a smart electronic machine, whereas packages and parcels were processed by postal workers who tossed them into a large rack of sacks, each one labelled by destination.

As Drew emptied the Wicksham Parva bag Penny distracted him briefly to say goodnight, presenting Ten Ends with the perfect opportunity to slip away unseen.

"Time to scarper," he whispered to himself. He turned, bolted across the floor and dived under a table.

It came as a bit of a surprise to find that his hidey-hole was already occupied by an old, rather portly, black labrador, which immediately let out a short, low, rumbling growl.

"Be quiet, Stanley, you silly dog," Drew shouted as he tossed another parcel into the sack labelled 'London', "or I shan't bring you to work in future!" Stanley whined in submission, then turned his attention to Ten Ends.

"He always uses Stanley when he's cross. I prefer Stan. Anyway, who or what are you?" He spoke quietly in animal tongue, well out of Drew's earshot, "I've never seen the like; and what on earth brings you in here?"

"I'm running away," Ten Ends whispered, and proceeded to tell Stan the wretched tale of his hapless adventure.

"Oh, I forgot to say. My name is Ten Ends."

"Funny name," Stan retorted quizzically.

"Yes. We were numbered rather than named. I'm the tenth child of Mr and Mrs Ends, doctor goblins from Tanglewood Deep."

Stan seemed sympathetic. "And where do you propose to go from here, young fellow?"

"For now, the further away from Tanglewood, the better."

"In that case I suggest that you jump into one of those sacks. I've heard my master Drew say that they are sent all over the country. The sorters go to the rest room in an hour's time for a cuppa. That's when you can sneak into one. I'll keep watch for you!"

Ten Ends thanked Stan for his help and waited for the sorters to go for their tea break. With a quick farewell to the friendly labrador, he scrambled out from beneath the table, jumped up on to the rack of sacks and leapt into a half empty one. It just happened to be labelled ...

'AIR FREIGHT – HEATHROW'.

His journey was only just beginning!

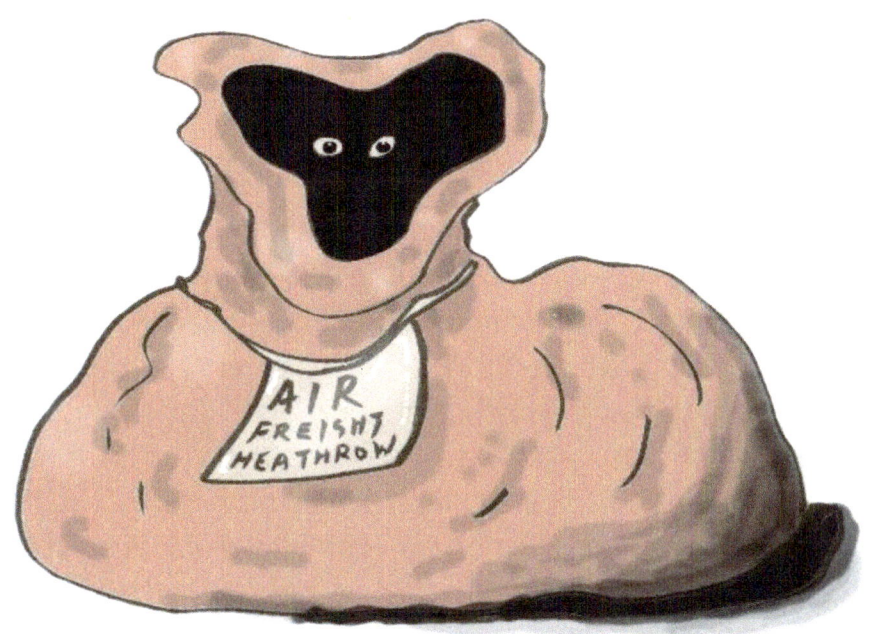

CHAPTER 2

FLEEING

Earlier that morning, just before Ten Ends had beaten his hasty retreat across the village green into the Wicksham Parva postbox, Ronald 'Clock' Robin flew up into a large oak tree near the pavilion to herald the spring dawn chorus and mark the approaching sunrise. His was always the first melody of the new day, hence his nickname 'Clock', though he was soon accompanied by a cacophony of birdsong from thrushes, blackbirds, wrens and all. Yet his daily timekeeping duties did not prevent him from observing and noting a small gnome-like figure scampering across the grass beneath him and disappearing into the large cylindrical red box so frequently visited by the humans. *"I wonder what that was all about?"* he thought to himself.

*****

Flight Sergeant Warwick Muldoon of the Feathered Air Force, more commonly abbreviated to the F.A.F., was busy tapping a new nest hole in a decaying oak tree when he received an early morning visit from the chief guardian of Tanglewood, the all-seeing, all-knowing Wye's Owl.

Muldoon, a great spotted woodpecker, had been promoted to the rank of Flight Sergeant after many years of service in aerial search and rescue. He was able to produce special patterns and variations with his long bill to tap out coded messages to birds in the locality or, on exceptional occasions, to transmit to a broader network of woodpeckers should a countrywide search be required. And Wye's Owl's request had an air of urgency about it!

"Wide area search please, Flight Sergeant! We have a missing doctor goblin, Ten Ends, believed to have been responsible last night for extensive damage in the village."

"Aye, aye, sir! I'll see to it straightaway!"

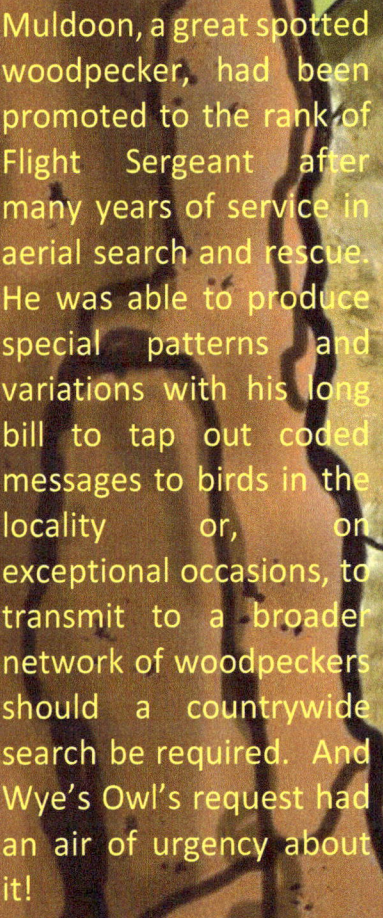

The daylight hunt for Ten Ends quickly got under way in Wicksham Parva yet, despite being extended to other nearby villages later in the afternoon, no sightings were reported, and the search was called off at dusk.

*****

During the night, the ill-fated goblin himself was enduring a bumpy ride in a mail sack carried from depot to depot until, early the next morning, a parcel lorry finally arrived at one of the distribution warehouses of London's Heathrow Airport. The sacks were taken inside the warehouse by forklift truck where they were emptied and sorted by destination. Later, the parcels would be loaded on to aeroplanes and despatched to the four corners of the earth.

As the contents of the sack concealing Ten Ends were tipped out, he managed to drop silently and unseen on to the floor of the warehouse. His heart was beating fast. Were he to be spotted by a human, he would surely be morphed into a garden gnome by The Shadow, Cobalus. Moving stealthily from one hiding place to another, he eventually managed to slip out of the warehouse through a side door and on to the vast expanse of the airport. To his surprise and advantage, very little activity was taking place. A widespread, thick fog had descended, and all Heathrow aircraft were grounded. He took the opportunity to move away from the main buildings and to find some dense scrub alongside one of the main lanes leading to Runway Two. At last, both hungry and frightened, he took cover by some machinery and sat down on an old concrete block to consider his next steps. Yet, in no more than a minute, he had curled up and fallen fast asleep. He had been away from his home in Tanglewood Deep for two long nights with barely a moment's rest.

By mid-morning, the fog had begun to lift when Ten Ends was rudely and suddenly woken from his slumber.

"Well, well, well! What have we here? A garden gnome?"

Ten Ends thought that his worst fears had come true, yet, far from being fossilised and lifeless, he found that he was able to open his eyes, turn around and look up.

"No, I do believe it's a goblin or even … judging by the size of its ears … yes! A doctor goblin!"

The powerful voice which addressed him emanated from the base of a large, bright orange forklift truck, whose headlights blinked as it beamed at the little creature before him.

"Good morning, little fellow. And what brings you to my patch? I haven't come across a doctor goblin since I met Loca, the dear little soul who brought me to life, but that's another story. So, what do they call you?"

"T-t-ten Ends, sir. You're right, I *am* a d-d-doctor goblin and I come from T-t-tanglewood in a village f-f-far away." Ten Ends had just woken up. The combination of the cold morning air and trepidation at the sight of the massive talking mechanism in front of him had together brought on an incontrollable stutter.

"M-m-may I ask who you are … … sir?" He added the 'sir' both out of politeness and fear. He had no desire to alienate this giant creature.

"Of course, you may, and do not be afraid. I shall not harm you. I am a working forklift truck, based here at the airport, although I was built in a place called Wiltshire. I lift heavy goods up on to aeroplanes. We're presently at a standstill because of the fog. Oh, yes, and my name is Guy ... Guy Fork."

"Don't the humans control you? Do they know you can talk?"

"Yes and no. They drive me around during the day when I perform my duties just like any other vehicle at the airport, but at night, out of sight, I have a life of my own. Only then do I talk," Guy chuckled. "A talking Fork, you might say!"

Ten Ends smiled and felt more at ease with his new companion. "So, you're like my friends Belinda and Bertie Brush. They're ordinary toothbrushes who walk and talk after dark. My neighbour, he's a doctor goblin too, used Cobalus to bring them to life. The trouble is that whenever I use Cobalus, things tend to go wrong."

"That says more about you than the power of Cobalus. Loca believed that doctor goblins should always have the best of intentions when using its power."

"That's what Doctor Locum told me. He's my distant cousin, the neighbour I told you about in Tanglewood, but I'm in his bad books at the moment. That's why I'm running away." Ten Ends then related the ill-fated events of the previous two nights, from the damage done by Handsome the lawnmower to his journey by post bag to Heathrow Airport.

Suddenly Guy butted in, "Did you say Locum just now? Doctor Locum? Well, grease my bearings! Loca had a boy called Locum. It's hardly a common name …" and, in turn, he proceeded to tell Ten Ends all about the doctor goblin called Loca Potion. He had spent his early days working in a factory yard on the edge of Savernake Forest where he had met her many years ago and when, as a test of her powers, she had used Cobalus to bring him to life.

"That's funny," thought Ten Ends after Guy had told his story, *"I never heard anybody in Tanglewood address Locum as Locum Potion."*

*****

Gossip was rife in Wicksham Parva that week. The villagers talked about nothing else other than the wanton destruction that mindless juveniles had caused with Farmer Jay's lawnmower. The animal population knew better, however, and the hunt for Ten Ends continued. The mischievous doctor goblin had been up to his tricks again. Eventually, a report had come in through the Feathered Air Force of a sighting on the village green. 'Clock' Robin flew over to Tanglewood in person to tell Wye's Owl and Doctor Locum that he had seen a goblin climbing into the postbox just as he, Clock, was heralding the dawn chorus the day before. "I thought it was strange at the time," he chirped.

Wye's Owl frowned on hearing the news. "That's not good, Locum. He daren't climb out in the daylight for fear of being seen. He would have been loaded in a sack by Penny Black when she made the afternoon collection yesterday, then taken to Markstow sorting office. After that ... who knows? By parcel post to any destination in the country, or even the world! The best we can do is to ask the sparrows roosting in the sorting office if they saw anything. Not that I hold out much hope for that!"

*****

Loca, a goblin of mature years, was in reflective mood as she sat in her armchair at home in the small surgery tucked away beneath a tree stump in Savernake Forest, Wiltshire. Nailed to the door was a sign which read 'Loca Potion, Principal Doctor Goblin'. Overall, she had enjoyed a long and happy life, and she still practised her healing powers on the sick and needy.

Sadly though, her husband had passed away a year or two earlier, but three of her four children and numerous grandchildren lived nearby and paid her frequent visits. She was never short of stimulating, kindhearted company. Yet the one great sorrow which still haunted her memory was being parted from her youngest son, Locum, a promising and gifted child, who simply disappeared one day whilst walking home from sprite school.

There were rumours that he had been swept away by a great golden bird, but these were soon dispelled, as the eyewitnesses were uncertain of their sightings and therefore considered unreliable. It remained a source of deep sadness and melancholy in Loca's heart, though not so much a mystery to her as it was to the rest of her family and friends!

*****

By mid-morning Heathrow Airport was simply buzzing with activity. Despite the fog, the terminals were chock-a-block with passengers eagerly awaiting their flights. The delays had meant that the shops and restaurants, too, were exceptionally busy. Outside on the concourse, passenger and freight planes were once more being refuelled and loaded. Guy Fork would soon be driven off to perform his daily tasks and was giving Ten Ends some last-minute advice and instructions.

"You must hide in the perimeter bushes, little goblin, until the planes stop flying just before midnight. I'll come back then and see if we can get you home. I don't yet know how, or the way to Tanglewood, but I have some friends who may be able to help. And for goodness' sake, stay away from the runways; planes can be extremely dangerous."

Ten Ends seemed thoughtful. "Guy, I have an idea. I'm not ready to face the music back home just yet. Instead, could

I go to that place where Loca Potion lives, you know … Snake Forest."

"Savernake," corrected Guy.

"If I could meet Loca, I could tell her all about my friend Locum, that he could just be her missing son. After which, when I return home, I'd have such good news for Locum that he'd forgive me for causing mayhem in the village. That's, of course, if I ever do find my way home," he remarked poignantly.

Just at that moment, Guy spotted his driver walking across to fetch him for the day's loading. He gabbled quickly and softly, "Now hide up till night-time, Ten Ends. I'll see if I can come up with something," then he froze rigidly back into a common or garden forklift truck.

Ten Ends scampered hurriedly away into some boundary undergrowth, an ideal place in which to hide. He soon found a soft tuffet of grass where he rested his head and, for the second time that morning, fell fast asleep.

*****

"Yes, twitter twitter, we saw him jump into a sack, then we heard one of the sorters say, 'That one's for Heathrow, Drew,' twitter, twitter. The sack was thrown into the back of the parcel van and off it went. We knew that there was an F.A.F. aerial search in progress and had stood by all night on full alert, twitter, twitter!"

Two overly excited, tweeting sparrows, Pip and Squeak, had flown in from Markstow sorting office, eager to report their sighting to Wye's Owl. Locum had stayed with Mr Tawny, incidentally a name used only by Wye's Owl's closest friends, to help plan the search and rescue operation. They praised the two sparrows for their vigilance and sent them on their way with grateful thanks.

Wye's Owl pondered. "Now if it WERE Ten Ends …"

"Who else could it have been?" Locum thought out loud.

"And IF they heard the word 'Heathrow' correctly …"

"Isn't that London's biggest airport?"

"And IF he's still there …"

"That's a lot of IFs," Locum muttered.

"Then I know someone who might just be able to help." Wye's Owl smiled with a faint hint of optimism. "I must get a message to Ducky immediately!"

"Ducky?", thought Locum.

*****

In the early afternoon two things jolted Ten Ends out of his slumbers. The first was hunger which was causing his stomach to rumble so loudly that a colony of ants felt the vibrations, came to investigate, and crawled all over him, inflicting the occasional bite. He could also hear dogs barking. The noise was coming from a nearby warehouse where a freight plane belonging to the Air Animal Commercial Airline was being loaded. And dogs meant food!

The hungry goblin decided to see what he could forage. He stood up, shook off a vast colony of busy ants, scratching his itchy legs as he did so, and set off in the direction of the warehouse, all the time concealed in the undergrowth. Peering through a gap in some crates near the entrance he was amazed at what he saw: dogs of many different breeds howling inside padlocked cages, a large collection of other animals, mostly pets, but also more exotic creatures such as chimpanzees, snakes and lizards, a mongoose, and even several great mammals, a leopard, a lion and lioness, a zebra and a large brown bear.

While the humans were focussing on the task of loading crates, cages and other boxes into the hold of a bulky freight plane, Ten Ends sneaked up to a cage in which a rather frightened brown and white spaniel sat disconsolately on a bed of straw. *'Here goes ...'* he whispered to himself.

"Hello, dog! What are you doing in that cage?"

The spaniel spun round, spotted Ten Ends and, by exercising both bravery and great self-control, managed to refrain from barking. Instead, she spoke softly in animal tongue, "We're being sent to Spain and I'm not dog, I'm Molly."

"Oh, and I'm Ten Ends, a very hungry doctor goblin from Tanglewood … Spain? Where's Spain?"

"It's where my owners are moving to. They say that it's really nice there by the sea, as well as being warm and sunny. But I just don't want to leave my lovely old house in Dorset. This plane will carry lots of pets like me, as well as zoo animals destined for a place they call a Bio Park."

Molly listened wistfully as Ten Ends, in turn, began to tell her all about his cosy little home in Tanglewood Deep and how much he regretted having to run away. Their friendly conversation was rudely interrupted as a forklift truck headed towards them to pick up the cage.

"Quickly! They mustn't see you. Squeeze through my bars and hide underneath me. I've got some dog food here you can eat."

Ten Ends needed little convincing, and in no time at all their crate had been lifted into the aeroplane along with all the other animal cages being transported to Spain. After a lengthy meal of Chewy dog meat, he squeezed out through the bars to talk to some of the other animals. None of them were there by choice. None of them wanted to be locked up. So Ten Ends made up his mind to help!

CHAPTER 3

FLYING

Before opening any of the cage doors, Ten Ends decided that if he wasn't going to get himself into any further bother, he'd have to tell all the imprisoned creatures to behave properly when they were released and not get involved in any of their usual in-fighting: cats scratching dogs, snakes spitting at mongooses, a lion chasing a zebra. Once he had found a way to open the cages and crates, they would have to dash to the rear loading door of the plane before take-off, jump out and scatter as fast as they could away from the airport.

But just as he was about to speak to them, he heard human voices coming from the flight deck into the rear hold. He dived for cover as the co-pilot and a veterinary steward arrived to secure the load and check the animals. When they were satisfied that everything was in order, the steward hung a large bunch of keys on a wall hook (incredibly GOOD news for Ten Ends) but then proceeded to close and fasten the rear loading door (extremely BAD news for Ten Ends), after which the two of them returned to the flight deck to prepare for take-off.

Before they knew it, the plane was taxiing to the end of the runway, the engines began to roar deafeningly and seconds later, they were climbing steeply into the sky. The escape plan had been thwarted. What's more, the animals in the hold were terrified.

Most of them had never experienced anything like this before.

Help! Let us out!" they cried. "Stop the plane! Open the doors."

Ten Ends, disregarding his own fear and displaying admirable courage, emerged from his hiding place and called for calm, but his little voice could not be heard above the roar of the jet engines. Slowly however, the plane reached its cruising altitude and levelled off. As the engine noise subsided, Ten Ends found himself alongside a huge cage containing a giant brown bear. This was someone with a very loud voice who could command the respect of all the other animals, the very creature he needed to win over as a useful ally.

FLYING

"Mr Bear, I need your help please!"

"Pardon?" the bear looked perplexed at the little creature peering through the bars. "You'll have to speak up. It's the engines. I can't hear you."

"CAN YOU HELP ME TO CALM DOWN THE OTHER ANIMALS, PLEASE." This time Ten Ends shouted at the top of his voice.

"NO NEED TO SHOUT. I'M NOT DEAF!" the bear bellowed. Then, more quietly, "I'll help if I can, but you'll have to get me out of here first."

Ten Ends knew that this was a risk, but he needed to rely on his instincts and put his trust in this giant furball. He must gain the bear's confidence.

"I'm Ten Ends," he cried, "and I'm a doctor goblin. And what's your name?"

"I am Sir Bagworth Brown." The bear had an aristocratic air about him. Suddenly he poked his giant paws through the bars of the cage. "A doctor goblin, eh? Do you happen to have any ointment on you, old boy? I've made my paws quite sore trying to bend these bars."

Fortunately, Locum had encouraged Ten Ends always to carry a few pills and creams in his waist pouch. 'You never know when you might need them', he'd say.

"Try this, Sir Bagworth." Ten Ends handed him a small bottle of lotion, which was emptied in seconds as the bear rubbed the cream into his paws.

"Most efficacious!" the bear exclaimed smiling. "Do you happen to have any more?"

Ten Ends shook his head apologetically.

"Never mind. Just let me out of here and tell me what you want."

Ten Ends hoped that he had done enough to gain the trust of this enormous beast and then remembered the bunch of keys. It was a real struggle for him to clamber up the wall and lift them off the hook. The larger keys were nearly as big as him, but he was eventually able to drag the bunch back to Bagworth's cage.

"It's likely to be one of the four biggest keys that will open your padlock, sir. I can't reach high enough, so you'll need to try the keys in turn with your paws through the bars."

As Sir Bagworth attempted to free himself, Ten Ends revealed his escape plan. "Before we release the others, we must tell them all to behave and be quiet. They will listen to you, and you can cuff them if they step out of line! We'll let them out for now, but as the plane lands they must all go back to their unlocked cages. When the steward returns to open the hold door, everything will appear to be under control, but while his back is turned, they can all make a dash for it."

Having successfully unfastened the padlock, Sir Bagworth Brown pushed open the cage door and emerged on all fours out into the hold. With a surprisingly swift pirouette, he unexpectedly swooped down and scooped up Ten Ends with his paw, at the same time standing upright and holding the horrified goblin high in the air for all to see.

Ten Ends was almost touching the roof of the fuselage and wondering what on earth was to become of him as the great bear asserted his authority.

"Listen, you chaps. Settle down and be quiet! I am Sir Bagworth Brown, a noble bear of the finest lineage and pedigree, and I therefore shall assume the right to take charge. Does anybody have a problem with that?"

The lioness opened her mouth to challenge Sir Bagworth but was quickly and firmly poked in the ribs by her mate. "Shut up and don't be a fool. This isn't the time to act the queen of the jungle. We're still in a cage, remember, and he's bigger than both of us put together." Then, addressing the other animals, he continued grovellingly, "I'm sure we all agree that Sir Bagworth Brown is just the person to lead our little band."

All the other animals immediately began to nod their heads.

"Well that's settled then!" Sir Bagworth presented Ten Ends to the four corners of the hold and continued his address.

"This little creature is a doctor goblin. He has great powers and has already treated my sore paw. He has an escape plan for all of us which you must listen to now. Ten Ends, tell them what to do!"

Ten Ends, who had been expecting the worst when Sir Bagworth had picked him up, now regained his composure and put his trust in the great creature. He stood up on the bear's outstretched paw and spoke as loudly as he could to his animal audience, outlining his escape strategy. The other animals listened intently as he spoke. He concluded his speech with a note of caution.

"If we let you out now, you must remain calm and quiet. No squabbling, please. You will then return to your cages for a short time as we land in Spain. Once the hold door is opened, you can all make your escape."

The animals nodded in unanimous agreement, signalling their approval of the plan. "Right ho! growled Sir Bagworth, "Now where did I put those keys?"

*****

All the time that Ten Ends was at large in Heathrow Airport and inadvertently boarding a plane en route to Spain, back in Tanglewood Wye's Owl had set in motion a Tawny Telegraph, known to the owls as T.T. A chain of tawny owls hooted messages from one patch of woodland to another in all directions, alerting the local squadrons of the Feathered Air Force and initiating aerial searches. The F.A.F. observers had been asked to pay particular attention to the area around London's Heathrow Airport, where they could expect help from a rather special team of birds …

*****

One by one Sir Bagworth Brown, ably assisted by his diminutive companion, Ten Ends, unlocked the cage doors and let the occupants out into the aircraft's hold. The animals were pleased to have some space, to stretch their legs and tails, as well as to meet and chat with some of their fellow passengers. On reaching their destination, Ten Ends felt proud that he would have presented the animals with a chance for the freedom they so longed for, although he was sad to think that he might never see his friends in Tanglewood again. How would he ever get back from Spain? Never mind, his escape plan appeared to be running very smoothly indeed. What could go wrong?

It all began when a small mouse which had eaten his way into a sack of straw in search of food, suddenly shot out across the floor of the hold. Instinct is a most difficult impulse to suppress, and a very lively tabby cat couldn't resist the temptation to give chase.

The flying mouser set all the dogs barking, and one excited pup in particular hared off after the cat. The other cats were now so agitated, they began to run for shelter and were pursued by even more dogs. The hissing, howling and barking stirred up a number of the zoo animals and, despite the best efforts of Sir Bagworth and Ten Ends to calm things down, the snake suddenly launched an attack on the mongoose and the lion started to growl at the zebra, while the lioness nipped Sir Bagworth's foot and called him a male chauvinist bear. Bagworth's response, a quick cuff round the whiskers, only served to reinforce her opinion.

The resulting effect of all this noise and frenzied movement was to alert the air crew. The co-pilot began to observe fluctuations on the dials of his instrument panel as the plane began to lurch and lose some stability. The veterinary steward thought he heard noises in the hold and decided to take a look. As he peered round the door into the animal section, he was horrified by what he saw. He slammed the door shut and rushed back to the flight deck.

"Skipper! The animals have all escaped from their cages. It's chaos back there, like a Disney cartoon. There's no way I can control the situation. It's much too dangerous to go inside without a team of handlers armed with harnesses and tranquilliser guns."

The pilot made an immediate decision to turn back.

"The plane is unstable, and we haven't yet travelled a quarter distance. Radio through to Heathrow immediately. Tell them to have all emergency services ready for our return, and that includes zookeepers, vets, animal charities ... the lot! We'll have to park up as far from the passenger terminal as we can. We don't want a member of the public being mauled by a lioness or bitten by a snake. Oh, and they'll need to fence off the area with some heavy-duty barriers before we open the hold doors in case any animal manages to slip away."

In no time at all, the plane was once again cruising down the runway at Heathrow, but this time on an inbound flight. Guided by staff on the ground and in the control tower, the pilot taxied the aircraft into a specially designated area, well away from the passenger terminals, and brought it to a standstill. The air crew sat back and gaped at the astonishing scene on the ground!

The place was throbbing with activity, with police organising a crowd of vets and animal handlers, men with tranquilliser guns, loaders pulling cages of all shapes and sizes and, much to the annoyance of all the airport staff, an army of reporters, photographers and T.V. personnel. How had they managed to get on the scene so quickly! Who had contacted them? The publicity would be disastrous for the Air Animal Commercial Airline and for Heathrow Airport itself.

The air crew were told to leave the aircraft immediately while the fences were put in place. Only when the area was fully sealed off and all the staff were ready, would the rear hold door be opened from the outside. Or so they thought!

Suddenly all the cameras were pointing at the aircraft as mayhem and panic ensued.

Loudspeakers issued warnings, flash bulbs flared, ambulances and fire engines rushed to the scene and people began to scream and shout. The hold doors were already open with a giant bear gripping the handle with its massive paws. Animals of all kinds were leaping from the plane, shaking themselves down from the steep drop and dashing off towards the gap in the barrier where the plane had entered. Before the escape route was sealed off, many of the speedier animals had already broken out, including a lioness, a zebra and a large number of cats and dogs, causing widespread alarm and fear. The enthusiastic press, however, were having a field day. There could be no doubt as to what that night's news headlines would be!

Amidst all the chaos, Ten Ends had jumped on Molly the Spaniel's back, lying flat to avoid detection, and she had scampered away quickly enough to slip through the closing barrier. He pointed her in the direction of the dense scrub where he had first met Guy Fork. Guy was, of course, still on loading duties. Ten Ends thought he'd wait there, as Guy had instructed, until midnight when the kindly forklift would return and, perchance, come up with some ideas. Molly, however, felt that she needed to get away from the airport as quickly as possible, so the two friends finally said their goodbyes and wished each other good luck. Perhaps one day they might meet again.

As Ten Ends sat down on his concrete slab, trying to make sense of the day's activities and wondering where he would go next, he suddenly found himself being lifted into the air, gripped in the talons of a great bird.

CHAPTER 4

DECISIONS, DECISIONS!

Ducky, the peregrine falcon, a member of the airport's Birdstrike Defence Team, was flying high above the runways at Heathrow with Ten Ends still held firmly in her claws. Her job was to scare away flocks of gulls and other birds which could cause aeroplanes to crash if they flew into the jet engines.

"We've been looking for you, young scamp!" Ten Ends, in his early twenties, didn't consider himself young, or a scamp. Goblins, so he believed, usually lived twice as long as humans and birds. "We received a message via Tawny Telegraph, hooted from a place called Tanglewood. We were requested to keep our eyes open for a troublesome doctor goblin called Ten Ends. I presume you are he?!"

"Er ... er ... yes! Ten Ends thought there was no point in denying it as doctor goblins usually inhabit woods and forests, not airports.

"And I suppose that you are responsible for the mayhem we can see below?"

Ten Ends looked down. The scene was more reminiscent of a battlefield in a safari park than a well-ordered, smoothly run international airport.

"Er … well … not exactly," Ten Ends spluttered, "I was just trying to help."

"Yes, I expect you were." Ducky's tone bore a note of sarcasm. "Now listen to me, Ten Ends! For your own good I'm going to keep you out of harm's way and drop you off somewhere safe, particularly with all that pandemonium going on down below. You could easily be spotted on the ground with humans trying to round up all those animals on the loose. Later, when the planes stop flying, I'll take you back to Guy Fork so you can sort out your problems with him. Meanwhile, I shall send a message to Tanglewood to say that I've found you, after which I really must get back to work."

"But who are you and where are you taking me?" Ten Ends looked nervously at the rapacious curved beak above him.

"I'm Ducky. It's short for duck hawk, another name for a peregrine falcon like me." Ten Ends started to giggle. He was expecting something a little more hard-hitting like Rocky, Blade or Flesh Eater.

"What are you laughing at?" growled the falcon.

"Er … nothing! I was just enjoying my ride. It's most exhilarating!"

"Well, we're here now." Ducky had taken Ten Ends to the highest point of the Heathrow control tower and set him down on its large circular flat roof, the size of a village bandstand. "This should keep you out of mischief. It's a long drop down there!" Ten Ends peered over the edge and went weak at the knees. "I'll be back this evening to pick you up."

Ducky flew off, leaving Ten Ends to sit and reflect on recent events and his own predicament. Evening was approaching and it would be the third night since he left his cosy little cottage in Tanglewood and went for that fateful ride on Handsome the lawnmower. Should he just try to get home and face the music, or venture on and go to Savernake Forest and look for Loca? Whichever path he chose, he'd need directions and a means of travelling long distances. But what if Ducky just left him there, stuck on top of the control tower? How would he ever get down? Whatever would become of him? He sat there, thinking … and began to feel very sleepy.

"I mustn't drop off," he thought, *"or I might … er …drop off!!"*

He chuckled to himself at his rather ill-chosen quip, but at least it kept him awake. If he stayed away from the edge, there was plenty of space to stretch his legs. He walked around the roof for a while, watching the planes take off and land.

On the concourse, the animal crisis appeared to be under control and flights had therefore resumed. At one point he thought he saw Guy loading baggage, but it could have been any one of numerous orange forklifts at work on the airfield. After an hour or so, just as the sun was setting and the control tower warning lights were switched on, his musings were suddenly interrupted by the arrival of a large black crow who immediately struck up a conversation.

"Good evening, Mister Goblin. How did you manage to get up here? Can you fly?"

"No. I was lifted up here by a falcon called Ducky." The very name caused him to start giggling again.

"No laughing matter," the crow explained, "She can be a brute when she's clearing the skies. We all keep well out of her way. I wouldn't put it past her to leave you up here simply because she doesn't like the look of your face or, even worse, to save you for her supper. I just wouldn't trust her. Anyway, what's your name and why were you left up on the control tower?"

The crow had sown seeds of doubt in the perplexed goblin's mind. "I'm Ten Ends and I'm a doctor goblin from Suffolk." Then, in his despair, he unexpectedly opened up to this stranger and began to pour out all his troubles, describing his encounters and escapades since leaving Tanglewood. "And I don't know whether to risk travelling home to face a frosty reception, or to try to find Savernake

Forest and Doctor Loca. There! I've told you everything and I don't even know your name."

"Stone the ravens," the crow exclaimed, "fancy that! I'm Clawdette Crow, by the way, at your service. I live in Chazey Wood, just an hour or so west of here, as the crow flies, of course. I like to stretch my wings in the morning, so I tend to fly to different places to feed every day. I've never heard of Tanglewood, though." Clawdette scratched her head thoughtfully. "It must be miles away, but, strangely enough, I know Savernake Forest well. It's an excellent source of food to the west of Chazey Wood. If you were to come home with me tonight, I could take you there tomorrow. I've finished here for the day. How about it?"

Ten Ends thought for a moment, weighing up his options. Who to trust, Ducky or Clawdette? Or neither? Decisions, decisions! Even with Guy Fork's help, there was no guarantee that he could find his way either to Tanglewood or Savernake Forest. Ducky's duties prevented her from leaving the airport. Alternatively, here was a chance to find Loca in the forest and redeem himself. Clawdette seemed friendly enough and he would, at least, be on the move. No waiting around for a falcon who might never return or spending another night at this barren airfield.

"Just one question, Clawdette. Is there anything to eat in Chazey Wood?"

"Everything to satisfy a hungry goblin's appetite," she replied fawningly, "buds, berries, grubs, worms … the lot."

She paused for a second or two. "Come on! Just hop on my back."

Ten Ends' mind was made up. He was on his way to Chazey Wood.

*****

As darkness fell, the seagulls and other birds that flocked around the airport flew off to their various night-time haunts to roost. Before she returned to her handler, Ducky quickly flew up to the top of the control tower to bring Ten Ends down to the paved area where, by this time, Guy would be parked up after finishing work in a nearby warehouse. On finding the little goblin missing, she immediately swooped down to land on Guy's roof instead.

"He's gone, Guy," she whispered in animal tongue, which sounded like bird chatter to his human driver. "I can't understand it. He could never have climbed down from there by himself. He must have had help. I'll get a message sent by T.T. We must tell Wye's Owl and Locum that we've lost him."

Guy deliberately misfired his engine to cover up his reply with a series of 'chug pops'. "He could still (chug pop) turn up at my overnight parking spot (chug pop). Nevertheless, (chug pop) tell them that he was planning (chug pop) to go to a forest in Wiltshire (chug pop), er... Savernake I believe, to find a doctor goblin (chug pop) called Loca Potion. It may just assist their search (chug pop)."

DECISIONS, DECISIONS!

At the steering wheel, Guy's driver had a puzzled look on his face and was scratching his head. *"That engine's making a funny noise,"* he thought. At that moment Ducky flew off the cab roof to find the local telegraph owl. Not long afterwards, unusual hooting could be heard in the night sky all the way from London to Tanglewood in Suffolk.

*****

Darkness fell and Clawdette flew over Reading with Ten Ends clinging firmly to her back and looking forward to his evening meal. Shortly afterwards they crossed a large country estate and dropped down into Chazey Wood where Clawdette's mate Clawed, a surly looking bird, was waiting impatiently on a branch next to their nest, high up in a spreading beech tree.

"You're late," he croaked sourly, "and I'm starving! You'd better have brought something decent. I'm fed up with road-kill."

"I thought you liked it. After all, you are supposed to be a carrion crow. Anyway, stop moaning. I've brought you a real treat, fresh goblin."

Ten Ends, startled, flew into a panic. He suddenly realised that he wasn't getting a meal, he was the meal! Without thinking, he leapt off Clawdette's back and fell about 10 feet onto a branch below and the frenzied chase began. The two crows took off and circled menacingly around the horrified goblin who, despite being winded after his fall, managed to run to the tree trunk and scramble down, frantically clinging to the bark with his tiny fingers. He was, fortunately, a very nimble goblin who had learnt the art of the swift getaway gleaned from his many misdeeds in the past.

At one point, Clawed Crow flew near enough to peck the tip of Ten Ends' left ear, but the terrified goblin managed to wriggle clear and scrape his way desperately down the trunk to the ground below, falling the last few feet into a bed of bluebells. When he finally picked himself up, he realised that he was trapped. The two crows had cornered him at the foot of the tree trunk and were closing in fast.

"Down here," a small voice whispered. "Follow me!"

Ten Ends turned to see a small whiskery nose and paw beckoning him down into a cavity between the roots of the

DECISIONS, DECISIONS!

tree. He didn't need to be asked twice. He dived into the hole and followed the rabbit, for that it was, his rescuer, down into the safety of its burrow.

Ten Ends found himself surrounded by half a dozen rabbits, both young and old. "Thank you, thank you!" he gasped, desperately trying to catch his breath. "I thought I was a goner. I trusted that Clawdette. She promised to give me a meal and to take me to Savernake Forest. How stupid I am, but that's the story of my life recently. I keep making the wrong decisions. How can I thank you enough?"

"Well now, little goblin, you can relax here and spend the night with us. Let me introduce myself. I'm Dug, leader of this warren and this is my family."

Dug proceeded to introduce them all by name. "My wife, Duchess, will take a look at that ear. It looks quite a nasty wound. We can also forage a little food for you, although we live mainly on grass. We know Clawed and Clawdette of old and tend to steer well clear of them. We have, in the past, lost several young buns to their talons, although not recently, with our excellent network of escape tunnels. But now you look as though you could do with some sleep. We'll wake you before dawn with breakfast, when you can tell us about your adventures and why you want to go to Savernake. I think we may just be able to help."

*****

Wye's Owl, high up in his oak tree hollow in Tanglewood, had received the T.T. message from Ducky in the middle of the night, but decided to wait until dawn to fly over to Tanglewood Deep and update Locum. The poor doctor had not been sleeping too well since Ten Ends had disappeared, so the kindhearted owl judged that he needed a good night's rest.

The following morning, Locum welcomed his visitor with a special concoction of cherry juice which perked them both up.

"Do we have any news, Mr Tawny? You said that Ducky had found Ten Ends at the airport. Is it possible to bring him home?"

"I'm afraid it's not good, Locum. Unfortunately, the bird, by which I mean our wayward doctor goblin friend Ten

Ends, has flown again, whereabouts unknown! He had, however, met a friend of Ducky, a Cobalus forklift truck called Guy. Guy told Ten Ends that he came from a place in Wiltshire, Savernake, where, in a nearby forest, he had been brought to life by a doctor goblin. Ducky didn't mention the goblin's name but did say that Ten Ends had a special reason to go there."

Locum fell suddenly silent, and a tear trickled from his eye.

"Did you say a forest near Savernake? I haven't heard that name for over forty years. It's where I was born!"

CHAPTER 5

THE GOBLIN WHO VANISHED

Every creature in the East of England had heard of Doctor Locum; his near neighbours knew him personally. He was the highly respected and eminent Principal Doctor Goblin from Tanglewood Deep. He had lived in his little tufted cottage for longer than any of them could remember and he had always been there to tend to their wounds, minister to their ailments and comfort the sick and elderly.

However, in truth, nobody really knew him at all. Where had he come from? Did he have any family or friends, apart from his mischievous neighbour, Ten Ends? What, if anything, did he do in his spare time? When and how did he learn to become a Principal Doctor Goblin? What was this great power, Cobalus, that he possessed, and where did it emanate from? He was, indeed, a strange and mysterious little fellow.

*****

On a cold, dull wintery afternoon some forty years earlier, Locum, just ten years of age, was walking home from sprite school by himself along a well-trodden path through Savernake Forest. The teachers were already aware of his exceptional talent and, as he often stayed behind for further tuition, his friends had gone ahead without him. Out of the darkening, twilight sky a huge golden bird had suddenly descended, grasping the little fellow in his talons, lifting him high and soaring far away towards the south Wiltshire chalk downs.

When he failed to return home from school, his mother, Loca, sent out her older children to look for him and soon the search had been extended forest wide.

Even the Feathered Air Force had been alerted. The only conceivable sighting had been reported by Chatty Patty, a small chiffchaff who thought she had spotted a golden eagle swoop down and snatch Locum away. Her account had been readily dismissed by other forest dwellers since golden eagles are never seen in the south of England, preferring a highland habitat. What's more, Chatty Patty, a bird who loved to gossip, had a bit of a reputation for embellishing the truth. Despite all the efforts of the various search parties, Locum, 'the goblin who vanished', was never again seen in Savernake Forest.

Cobalus, The Shadow, an energy source which radiates outwards from the standing stones of the ancient Wiltshire monument of Stonehenge, is absorbed in the soul of every doctor goblin in all the woodlands of the country. Yet the natural character, integrity and intellect of the individual goblin determines the effectiveness of their use of this power. Locum had been singled out as an exceptionally gifted and talented youngster. He was destined to become a great healer, but first he must undergo a long and difficult apprenticeship, one of the 'Chosen Few'. The golden bird which had abducted him from Savernake Forest was Cobalt, a ghost eagle, the messenger of Cobalus. This huge, mystical creature, invisible to humans, but occasionally spotted by other birds and animals, was there to do the bidding of his master. He had been instructed to bring Locum to Stonehenge. Dropping him right into the centre of the great stone circle, he flew to rest on top of one of the massive lintels.

Locum was confused at first, frightened and tearful. *'Where was he? What was that bird? Why has he dropped me here? Why hasn't he tried to eat me?'*

"Be at peace, Locum! You have nothing to fear. There is no safer place for you in the whole, wide world." The voice he heard emanated from a shimmering, hazy apparition. It was both deep and kind, strong, though reassuring, soft, but also commanding.

"I am Cobalus, The Shadow, your spirit, your power, your energy. I will always be with you, but you have much to learn. You will leave behind your old life to do great things.

Your family will lose you, but the poor, sick and needy will always find you. You have a great task to fulfil for which you must now prepare and train."

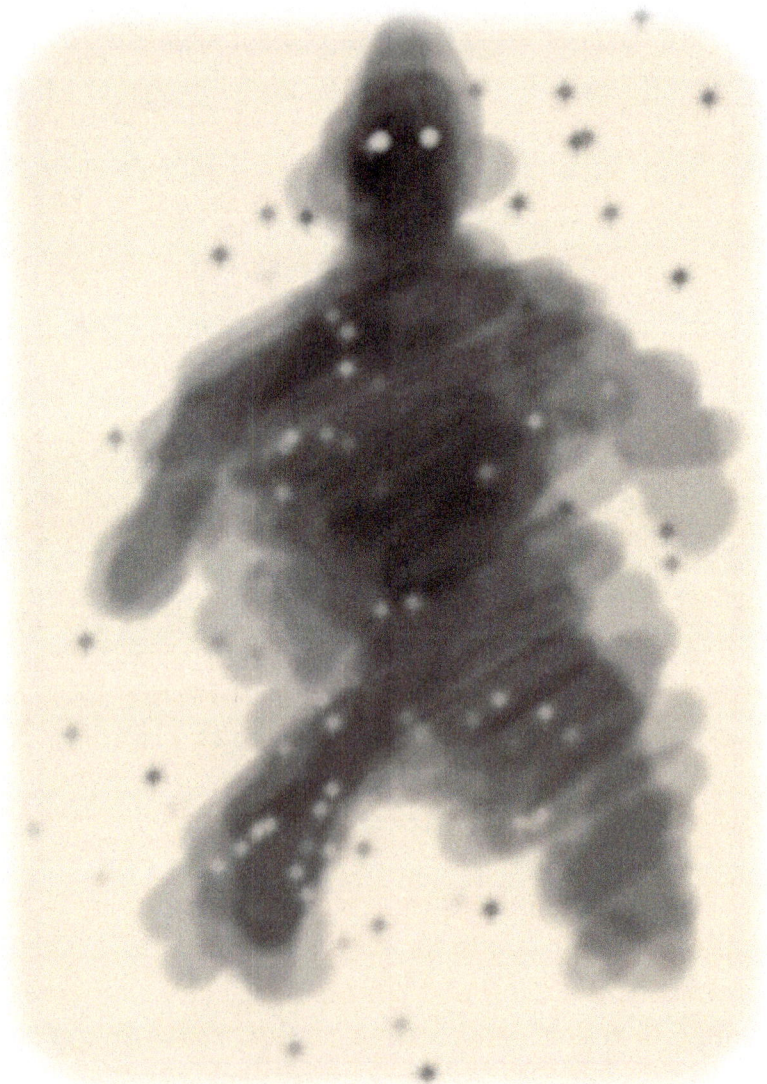

Strangely enough, Locum had always known that he was different from his sister and two brothers. He wasn't like his school friends either, although they accepted him for who he was, recognising his special qualities. After the initial shock of his earlier abduction, he suddenly felt that he was meant to be here, that he was destined to follow a different path and, as he sat up and looked out between the stones of the great circle, an overwhelming calmness came over him and he was at peace with the world round about.

Locum's training would last twelve years. Cobalus had divided the country into eleven regions properly known as Principalities, as each was overseen by a Principal Doctor Goblin who had been selected and trained in the same way. Locum would spend a year in each Principality, immersing himself in the history, geography and customs of that region, as well as gaining knowledge of every medicine, potion and treatment used in the goblin realm. Finally, in his last year of study he would return to Grovely Wood, near Stonehenge, where three elderly, retired and highly revered principal goblins, the Cobalus Professors, would put him through a series of challenging tests designed to ensure that he, Locum, was indeed ready to become a fully qualified Principal Doctor Goblin.

It is at this point in Locum's career that we pick up his story. He had studied hard and travelled widely over eleven years in each of the Principalities, carried from one region to another by Cobalt, the ghost eagle.

Now a young man of twenty-two years, Locum was living with four other year 12 student goblins in 'the hollow trunk which never rotted' at the heart of Grovely Wood.

The five students were given no time at all to settle in and get to know each other before the final year's testing began. On the contrary, it was obvious from the start that they were highly likely to be in competition with each other. The early tests were straightforward. The five apprentices were thoroughly examined over a three-month period by each of the three Cobalus Professors in turn. The first term covered the customs, history and folklore of the eleven Principalities, including the behaviour of life forms other than humans, animals and goblins. They investigated the world of witches, gremlins and trolls, indeed, all the creatures of folklore. In the second of the four terms their knowledge of geography was put under scrutiny. What did they know about the forests, mountains and rivers of the Principalities? What were the habitats of the creatures who lived in them? Where might elves and sprites be found? What spirits might exist in the lakes and streams?

The Cobalus Professor who tutored them in the third term was a goblin called Fleur who rigorously examined their knowledge of medicine, covering every subject from potions and pills to the treatment of sickness and injury. Locum was surprised that a female doctor goblin had become a professor and, at a private moment, even plucked up the courage to ask if it had been harder for her to become a Principal Doctor Goblin and, furthermore, a Cobalus Professor than it would have been for a male goblin. Her reply astounded him: "You should have asked your mother. She is one of the finest Principals in the country. It was she who put you forward for training!"

With just one term of their twelve year's training to be completed, the five apprentices were flown back to Stonehenge. After a two-day break, they were summoned to the centre of the stone circle where, at midnight on a full moon, they were addressed by the voice of Cobalus.

"You, the Chosen Few, have all done well, succeeding in every area of study and have all, therefore, earned the right to participate in the final two tests. This is not surprising as, years ago, you were recommended and selected for training by the principal of your region. You have all demonstrated your capacity to retain knowledge. The last two trials, however, will be tests of your character, your compassion and your courage. But first, what you have all been waiting for … your scores!

"*Elfric, Principality of Mercia: 87 out of 100*
Rysbottom, Principality of The Ridings: 89 out of 100

McBrownie, Principality of Caledonia: 92 out of 100
Locum, Principality of Wessex: 95 out of 100
And finally, Tomos, Principality of Cambria: 96 out of 100"

The standard of all your performances was exceptional. Only 9 marks separated you and only Tomos' superior knowledge of the wild Cambrian landscape enabled him to pip Locum by just one point.

And now for your final two tests. The first of these will test your compassion and ingenuity. You will each be dropped into one of five different towns under the cover of darkness, where you will remain for ten days. You will be given no food or drink. You must fend for yourselves. If you are seen by a human in the daylight, you will be petrified and take the form of a garden gnome. I'm sure that the finder will be delighted to have a shiny new ornament watching over their garden pond!

You must use the power of Cobalus to bring to life two inanimate objects. One can be as large as you deem to be useful and sensible. The other must be small, less than your own height and weight. Both must be used for the benefit of all living creatures and on that measure alone you will be marked.

You will all be dropped off by Cobalt tomorrow evening. Now rest, consider the task ahead, and work out your strategy. Away you go."

At this point, Elfric, the Mercian apprentice, raised his hand. "Lord Cobalus, you said that there were two tests. Can you tell us what the other one is?"

But all that could be heard was the wind whistling through the giant stones.

*****

It took a few seconds for a sleepy Ten Ends to remember that he had spent the night in an underground rabbit warren from which Dug and Duchess, his rescuers and kindhearted hosts, had already ventured out, foraging in the undergrowth to provide their guest with a small, but nourishing breakfast.

Ten Ends was on his best behaviour. "You're very kind," he spluttered, with his mouth full of pips and berries. "I cannot thank you enough for rescuing me from those vicious crows last night. I thought I'd had it! But did I hear you say that you might be able to help me get to Savernake Forest?"

Dug smiled at the ravenous little goblin. "Yes indeed, Ten Ends, but first you must eat your breakfast and take it easy for the remainder of the day. We cannot travel safely until dusk, when we shall accompany you from here, warren by warren, to Savernake. Each warren will provide its own guide. They are quite used to escort duties. We rabbits are extremely poor fighters, so we stay away from trouble and tend to know all the safe routes across country. Many animals and goblins have used us as guides. However, be prepared for a long journey. Even if we carry you, it will take three nights to reach the great forest."

The pair journeyed all night from Chazey Wood to another small copse some ten miles away. To give Dug a break, Ten

Ends would occasionally jump off his back and run as fast as his little legs would carry him.

At dawn, after a tiring night's journey they reached their destination, a large warren where Mike, Dug's cousin and Ten Ends' host and guide for the second leg of the journey, welcomed them both with food and a soft hay bed for the day's rest. But at nine o'clock that morning the rabbit on watch duty heard the ominous sound of human footsteps approaching the western burrow and immediately alerted Mike and his guests. They all hoped that the humans were harmless ramblers out for a day's walk but, as a precaution, sent scouts along every entrance tunnel to see if they could spy any activity outside.

"Purse nets! Purse nets!" The cry rang out from several of the scouts. "Prepare for ferret attack!"

"What's happening?" Ten Ends cried.

"They're netting our tunnel entrances," Mike explained. "In a moment they'll send a ferret down to chase us out into the nets. All of you! Run down to the emergency burrow. I'll back in last, block the entrance and face the ferret, while you all hide behind me. He is a long beast and will have difficulty turning around. That will give us precious time while his owner is forced to dig him out. At that point they might even give up. Whatever you do, don't run to the exit burrows."

"How can I help?" Ten Ends wanted to repay these gentle creatures for their kindness to him.

"Have you ever encountered a ferret before?"

"No, Mike, but I have faced a stoat. Just leave the blighter to me!"

All the rabbits, young and old, had been herded into a large, deep hollow with just one narrow entrance. This was being blocked by Mike, a large and powerful buck rabbit, who crouched there bravely, ready to die if needs must, anything to protect his family. Dug stood just behind him prepared to step in should Mike be overcome. However, strangely enough, the first line of defence was Ten Ends, who was kneeling down in front of Mike with a seriously determined look on his face.

There was a long and tense wait but eventually the ferret, following his nose, caught a strong scent and appeared around the corner where the rabbits were hiding. Baring his sharp teeth into a scornful smirk, he peered through the gloom and spotted Mike's large upright ears. He hadn't noticed the diminutive figure crouched between Mike's legs. Without warning he rushed at the brave, frightened rabbit. The last words the ferret heard were 'Cobalus Freeze!', before he fell like a plank to the floor of the tunnel.

Ten Ends, having used a powerful Cobalus spell to protect the rabbits, took control. "Dug, Mike, drag him right down into the emergency hollow for now. He'll be frozen stiff for at least a couple of hours. Tell the rabbits to come out and make their way to the eastern tunnel exit. I'll go ahead and loosen the purse net while the humans are hanging about at the western end. You can all get away and hole up for the time being in any old disused warren further into the copse. The humans will be digging their ferret out for a long time yet. They'll get a surprise when they find him!"

Within the safe confines of the abandoned warren, the rabbits rested for the remainder of the day, all of them hugely grateful to Ten Ends for their seemingly miraculous escape. The little goblin himself was pleased that he had, for once, used the power of Cobalus to help others and with such a beneficial outcome.

At dusk, after a day's rest, Dug departed to return to Chazey Wood and Mike set off with Ten Ends in the direction of Savernake Forest.

The final stages of Ten Ends' journey were long, tiring, though fortunately uneventful, and at dawn on the fourth morning, he said goodbye to his third rabbit guide and stood, in the half light, looking up at the daunting mass of giant trees in front of him. He urgently needed to find cover where he could rest and hide up for the day before setting out on his search for Doctor Loca.

Cautiously entering the forest along a narrow animal track, he walked for nearly an hour before spotting a large hollow log lying hidden in the undergrowth.

"Just the job!", he thought and peered inside. All he could see in the darkness was a pair of large white eyes. The creature emitted a terrifying howl and slithered slowly and threateningly towards him.

CHAPTER 6

SHASTON

It was midnight in the spring month of April and the last year of Locum's training. The five apprentice doctor goblins, the 'Chosen Few', sat nervously in the centre of the ancient Stonehenge megalithic circle waiting to be transported to their respective west country towns. The voice of Cobalus had reminded them of their task: ten days fending for themselves; always out of human sight; bringing two objects to life for the benefit of others.

Cobalt, the ghost eagle, had been observing the proceedings from the top of a massive stone lintel. After the voice of Cobalus had faded away and without further warning, he suddenly took off and hovered above them. Spreading his wings wide and raising his head to the sky, he began to clone himself until, on both sides, he was flanked by two other ghost eagles. In perfect formation, the five mystical birds suddenly swooped down and whisked the young goblins away.

There are now five tales to tell, yet we shall dwell on just one, as we follow the young apprentice Locum to the town of Shaston in North Dorset, for it was here that the ghost eagle had set him down, at midnight, amidst the ruins of an ancient abbey. The low stone foundations were, for the most part, the abbey's only remaining fragments, while the ground in between was laid to lawn with flower borders. Public seating afforded splendid views over the Blackmore Vale below, for the town itself stood on a high chalk hill. The gardens offered an element of security, as they were devoid both of humans and street lighting. Locum was quickly able to find a corner of the ancient building where the walls were a little higher and provided shelter on two sides. He sat down on the grass to reflect on his task and consider his next move.

Before long he would need to eat, although, with April showers, water should not be a problem. Despite the risk of discovery, he felt he should also observe human activity in daylight, their meeting places, their vehicles, their shops, their everyday needs. Only by doing so would he know how to help them using his Cobalus powers. Or should he forget humans and concentrate on his own natural world, animals, birds, and what some would call creatures from folklore, in which category he himself belonged? The task would certainly be easier as he could then operate in the relative safety of darkness.

Yet this was meant to be a challenge, a test of character, and it was no coincidence that the apprentices had all been dropped off in towns. He knew he must not take the easy option. He must learn about humans. While still under cover of darkness, he decided to venture out and explore this man-made settlement more thoroughly. Leaving the safety of the abbey garden, he set off along an adjacent footpath towards a glow of light some 200 yards distant. In a few minutes he had reached the town centre. As well as streetlamps, a few lights in windows suggested that not all human life had shut down for the night. Hanging from one large building was a sign embellished with a picture of a half moon.

Locum could hear singing coming from within. Occasionally an unsteady human would emerge from the building, forcing him to take cover behind a dustbin, postbox or doorstep.

Eventually, as he sprang from one hiding place to another, he noticed that nearly every light had been switched off, and the humans had retreated indoors for the night. When all seemed quiet, he grew bolder. Turning into a side road, to his great surprise, he came across a fox tearing into a plastic waste bag.

"Some good pickings here," the fox remarked. "These humans don't half waste food. Anyway, you're a doctor goblin, aren't you?" There was little expression and no malice in his voice. Foxes knew that these little creatures had greater powers than a sharp set of teeth. "Hardly your territory."

"And hardly yours," replied Locum, who was more used to seeing foxes in hedgerows and woodland.

"More foxes in towns and cities these days. The food is, so to speak, in the bag! No more creeping up on chicken runs for me. No more pellets in my backside from a farmer's shotgun. If the humans spot me, I simply slink off home. Apart from the messy bins, I think they have a soft spot for me!"

Introductions followed. Luey, the fox, lived underneath a store shed behind the high street greengrocer's shop. After Locum had told his story, describing the trial he was currently undergoing, the friendly fox kindly invited him to spend the next ten days with him at his humble home.

"You'll be safe there, and you'll enjoy a feast of different meals, vegetable peelings, apple cores, banana skins, bread crusts, fried chicken bones, half eaten burgers, the lot. There's a freshwater pond in the back garden, so plenty to drink. You could even have a midnight skinny dip."

"Perhaps not," Locum muttered to himself with raised eyebrows, but his task had suddenly become considerably easier. "You're most kind, Luey. How will I ever repay you?"

"No need for that. Your company will be enough. Mind you, the cubs tend to have the occasional injury or chill but nothing to really test your medicinal skills! Come on, let's go home."

Underneath the store shed, Locum was introduced to Sammie, Luey's mate, and her four small cubs. She quickly served up a meal of scraps on two bark plates for Luey and his guest.

"If you're going to observe human behaviour in the daylight, you'll need a good hideout in a busy spot. I'll put on my thinking cap. Now get some rest; we'll need to make an early start in the morning."

*****

The sun was still well below the horizon when Luey and Locum crept out from under the store shed and along the side path to the front of the greengrocers. The main shopping precinct in Shaston centred around two large historic buildings, the Town Hall and the adjacent St. Peter's church, in front of which stretched a broad pedestrian pavement. On it stood a post box, bench seating, a number of bollards marking off the edge of the busy road, a signpost with arms pointing towards the town's main tourist features and three large square tubs containing a rich and colourful array of tall spring flowers.

"There's your hiding place, Locum, but you will have to tuck down amidst the plants very soon now. The greengrocer sets up his front display long before the shops open. Daily life begins early here, with postmen, shop workers, milkmen and window cleaners to name but a few, and, of course, it must be after dark before you creep back to the shed. Nevertheless, you'll get an excellent view of life in the town centre. This will help you decide on the two objects you mentioned."

Sammie had packed up a lunch bag for Locum. "And here's a little cup; you'll get plenty to drink when they water the plants." She paused and chuckled, "And a good soaking too!"

"Thank you, Sammie. I'll creep in after dark and try not to disturb the cubs." With that, the little goblin set off cautiously for the flower tub, keeping under cover as far as possible and making sure that he wasn't seen.

From his floral hiding place, Locum spent the morning quietly observing human behaviour. He was fascinated by the way they went into buildings with large windows to forage for their food, how they all wore different clothes in a variety of colours, how the mothers pushed their children around in boxes on wheels and how they spent a lot of their time avoiding large cars and buses as they crossed the road.

As Sammie had predicted, he received a soaking mid-morning when a man from the council came to water the tubs, but he managed to stay out of sight and fill his drink cup. He spent some of the long daylight hours contemplating how he would use the power of Cobalus. *"What objects, one large and one small, could I bring to life which would bring some benefit to these humans?"*

As he began to make a mental list, his train of thought was suddenly and dramatically interrupted by a long deafening screech followed by a dull thud. He stared out across the street and was horrified at the scene directly in front of him. A small boy had run out into the road and had been knocked over by a long, white, single-decker bus.

The traffic stopped and a large crowd quickly gathered around the child. Locum, with the instinct and training of a good doctor, and with no thought as to his own safety, leapt out of the flower tub and, while the numerous spectators were distracted by the incident, he shot across the road unobserved and dived under the bus just behind the front wheels.

Moving forward, he looked ahead and saw the injured boy lying right in front of him surrounded by a rapidly growing crowd. As Locum could only see their legs and feet, he reasoned that they would, conversely, be unable to see him. The wounds looked bad, however. Both legs seemed twisted and broken, while blood oozed from a large gash on the back of his head. He was also very, very still …

Without even considering the consequences of his actions, Locum, with intense concentration, focussed his eyes upon the child, rubbed his ears resolutely and invoked the life-giving power of Cobalus. Within seconds, the boy's legs straightened, his head wound faded away and he opened his eyes to see Locum staring at him!

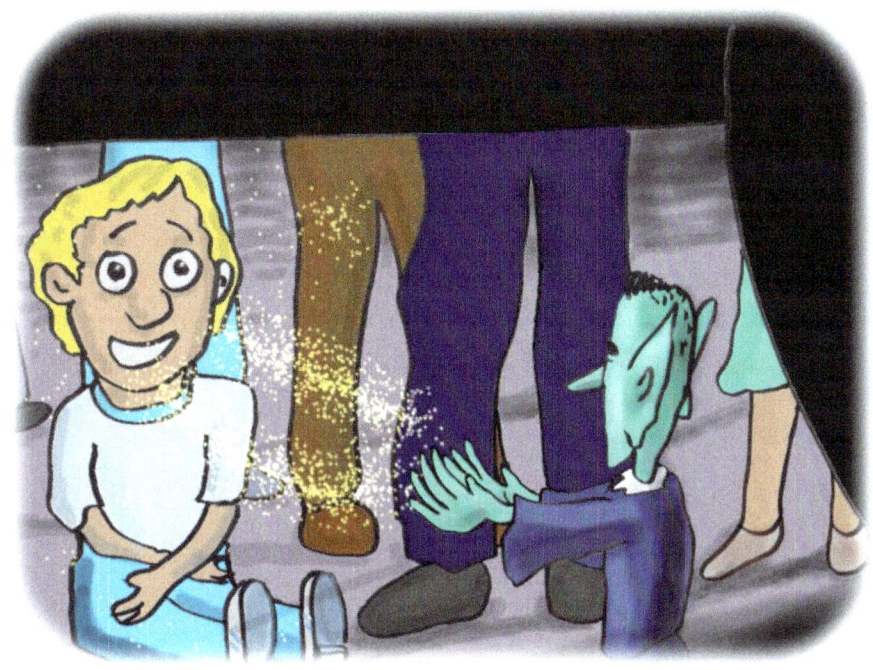

The onlookers gasped with amazement. They had seemingly witnessed a miracle. The bus driver was shaking with a mixture of shock, anxiety and relief. The boy's mother was in floods of tears as she hugged her child to her. Soon first aiders, a doctor and a police car were on the scene and the boy was checked over. There seemed to be absolutely nothing wrong with him, but he would have to go to hospital for tests and an x-ray. He then looked directly into his mother's eyes and exclaimed firmly and clearly so that all about him could hear, "Mum, it was a goblin; a goblin brought me back to life." As the onlookers stood marvelling at the child's incredible recovery as well as his vivid imagination, *(Goblins indeed!),* Locum realised with horror that he had been seen by a human in daylight. He felt the strength passing inexorably from his limbs and body, while his mind, slowly but surely, began to close down.

When the police had cleared the road and the coach had been driven away, a local traffic warden found a garden gnome close to the kerb and took it home to place on the rockery next to her garden pond.

It was providential that the Cobalt ghost eagles who had delivered the five apprentices to the towns selected for their individual trials, had been ordered by The Shadow to monitor their activities and to report back to Stonehenge if anything should go amiss.

*****

Over the ten days of the trial, each of the other four apprentices had stuck to their tasks, stayed clear of danger and had eventually been flown back by ghost eagle to Grovely Wood. Here, they met the three Cobalus Professors whose task it was to assess their experiences and to consider the objects into which they had breathed life. At this point they were told that one of their number had, unfortunately, failed to complete his tasks and that an announcement would be made later at Stonehenge by Cobalus, The Shadow. One of the apprentices was certain that he had overheard a conversation in which a professor had used the words 'garden gnome'. The professors then listened to the apprentices as, in turn, they described their ten-day trials and detailed the objects they had chosen. Their accounts would be assessed and awarded a mark out of fifty.

Elfric of Northumbria had chosen a step ladder which had allowed him to climb walls and reach heights from which he could observe human behaviour. His small object was a tin opener, which not only brought him canned food from shops and kitchens while he himself remained out of sight, but it also opened the tins to provide both himself and others in need with a source of food. *(43 marks awarded.)*

A living lamppost was Rysbottom of The Ridings' choice. While in its usual location during the daytime, at night it would come alive, when it could be used by its doctor goblin for illuminating any place or activity where light was needed. His cleverly chosen small object was a multi-purpose pen knife. With a life of its own, there would be a multitude of situations where it could be of benefit to others. *(46 marks awarded.)*

McBrownie of Caledonia had opted for a twenty-pound note and a bicycle. He dropped the note on the street for people to find and spend, and later, when the coast was clear, the note would run back to him for the process to be repeated. Whereas this had been of benefit to the finder, it left the vendor with a £20 shortfall in their takings. The bicycle was an even less successful choice, as nobody in town wanted to take it away without permission, so McBrownie used it at night to take himself for rides. *(37 marks awarded.)*

The leading apprentice, Tomos from the Welsh Principality of Cambria, had instilled life into a dustbin, which at night would be guided by Tomos to travel the streets picking up all the rubbish before taking it to the recycling centre. Visitors to the town would remark on its absence of litter, the residents praised the council dustmen for their excellent endeavours, while the dustmen themselves scratched their heads in disbelief. Tomos' small object was a door key. Once alive it could flex itself into a shape to open any door. *'How useful is that!'* Tomos supposed. *(45 marks awarded.)*

After the Cobalus Professors had made their final reckoning, both they and the apprentices were taken back to Stonehenge by Cobalt and his ghost eagles. The four apprentices were seated in a row on a fallen stone as the voice of Cobalus addressed the gathered band. The atmosphere became somewhat subdued when they were given the full details of Locum's tragic parting, although Tomos noticed that Cobalt had flown away as the announcement was made.

The marks for the ten-day town trial were added to their previous test scores, establishing an order of merit. Lusor, the senior Cobalus Professor, read out the updated scores out of 150:

> *"Tomos, still in first place with 141 marks.*
> *Rysbottom, who has jumped from 4th to 2nd place, with 135.*
> *Elfric, up from last to third, with 130.*
> *Finally, McBrownie, with some rather strange object choices, who scores 129."*

When Professor Lusor had sat down, the voice of Cobalus quietly addressed the apprentices.

"All four of you, the Chosen Few, have performed well in your first trial and your long, twelve-year training programme is nearly over. You will now advance to your final and most challenging ordeal, after which two of you will immediately be awarded the title of Principal Doctor Goblin. The others will be titled Assistant Principals. All this, of course, assumes that you manage to get through the final trial.

You will be taken west, to the Great Oak Forest of Dean, which, in itself, will present many unimaginable threats and dangers for you. But it also happens to be the mysterious and unnerving dwelling place of the witch, Ypsilon Thrubb. You will be set down at the forest edge in intervals of an hour, in the reverse order of your latest scores. So McBrownie will lead out, with Tomos leaving last. Your task, which will test your ingenuity, your skills, but most of all, your courage, will be to bring me back the wand of Ypsilon Thrubb!"

There were gasps all around. Ypsilon Thrubb had a fierce and malicious reputation, a witch with supernatural powers almost equal to those of The Shadow himself, except that she used her magical spells for the most evil of purposes. This was a frighteningly dangerous mission which could easily lead to loss of life.

The voice of Cobalus continued. "Do not be afraid. If you show courage, determination and resourcefulness, I shall be with you. You will only be in danger if you fail to demonstrate these qualities."

"Oh, and Locum, you will be the fourth of the five apprentices to enter the forest."

The other apprentices spun round in sheer amazement. Cobalt had dropped Locum, alive and well, to the grassland just behind them.

"Disregarding his own safety, Locum was turned to stone, having been seen by the human child whose life he had so gallantly saved. I, Cobalus, The Shadow, have therefore chosen to breathe life back into him. He will participate in the final trial."

CHAPTER 7

LOOKING FOR LOCA

"I'm so sorry. I didn't mean to disturb you … er … whatever you are. I was just looking for somewhere to shelter for the night and I saw your log. I'll leave immediately … er … straightaway … er … terribly sorry!"

Ten Ends turned to run out of the hollow tree trunk where he had hoped to rest during the day before continuing at dusk with his quest for Doctor Loca, hidden away somewhere in Savernake Forest.

"Wait!", the creature bellowed. "If my weary eyes do not deceive me, I'd say you are a doctor goblin. Am I right?"

Ten Ends hesitated. "Er … yes … er … I am a doctor goblin. Why do you ask, Mister … er … Mister …?"

"I'm not Mister, or Missus come to that. I am Squirm, an extremely large, you may say giant, and incredibly old earthworm, and you have disturbed my beauty sleep. Now these days I prefer to snooze above ground. All that subterranean digging sets off my rheumatism. Well, while you're here, you can make yourself useful, especially if you want a place to bed down for the night. Now, Doctor … er … what's your name, what have you got for my aches and pains?"

"Ten Ends."

"Ten Ends? Ends of what? How will these ends help my rheumatism?"

"No, Ten Ends, that's my name! I'll take a look in my pouch … I have some Fruits of the Wood cream here. It's made from willow bark. That should do the trick. Mind you, it's such a small pot and you're such a fa …er, enorm … er …" At this point Ten Ends, not wishing to cause offence, felt the need to correct himself. "… such a well-built fellow … er … lady … er … thingie, that this will run out very quickly. You need to get a repeat prescription from your local doctor goblin. Speaking of which, I believe that there is an excellent female practitioner here in Savernake by the name of Loca Potion?"

"Yes, I've heard of her. She lives far across the forest to the north, much too long a journey underground for me at my age. Anyway, as Principal Doctor Goblin she is responsible for the whole Principality and would be far too busy to see little old me. No, I'll go and see Tam-Van. He's our local doctor goblin and lives in an underground surgery not a stone's throw from here. He's very good and, I'm told, a bit of an expert on infectious diseases. We had a nasty outbreak of mole flu a few years back which caused a number of fatalities in the subterranean population. He soon had that under control. He eventually developed a potion which prevented it from spreading, but before that we all had to wash in rainwater and stay a worm's length apart. Mind you, he didn't say what type of worm. Nobody came near me for weeks."

As Squirm finished talking, he looked down at Ten Ends who had fallen fast asleep on the soft bark floor of the log. The old worm smiled to himself before settling down for his own daytime nap.

*****

"Don't forget to go and see Doctor Tam-Van. Ask for Fruits of the Wood cream. Oh, and thanks for letting me spend the day in your log shelter, Squirm. I shan't forget your kindness."

Ten Ends' parting words as he set off at dusk on his journey to the north of Savernake Forest were met with a wriggly wave from Squirm and a cheery 'Good luck, Ends!'

Goblins, like most supposedly mythical creatures, are generally nocturnal. Unlike humans, they feel safer under the cover of darkness. Trudging through the forest undergrowth, Ten Ends had two main concerns; he was both very hungry and he had no real way of knowing in which direction he was travelling. The forest canopy prevented navigation by the stars and the tracks through the trees twisted and turned so much that he quickly realised that he had no idea where he was. After passing the same ancient, knurled oak tree for the third time, he decided to sit down, get his bearings, and consider his next steps. However, following a few moments of focussed but unproductive thought, his mind began to wander as the hopelessness of his quest gradually dawned on him. It was then, from above, he heard the singing.

LOOKING FOR LOCA

♪ Sweetest song you ever heard,
Lady Lucy, ladybird,
Underneath the Compass Tree.
Which direction? Just ask me!
Sweetest song you ever heard,
Lovely Lucy, ladybird. ♪

As Ten Ends looked up, a bright red ladybird, the size of a small apple, landed on his lap.

"Lost, are we? Lady Lucy at your service!"

"Oh! Er …" Taken by surprise, Ten Ends found himself, not for the first time, at a loss for words. "How did you know I was lost?"

"Because you are sitting under the Compass Tree. You must be wearing metal. There! Your belt buckle."

"Why yes! It's an old washer I found in Farmer Jay's barn. So what?"

"The Compass Tree has a magnetic field. If you're lost and wearing metal, you are drawn towards it. After you've passed it three times, it calls me. I happen to be magnetic, too. I then show you the way."

"But how? And who or what are you?" Ten Ends seemed mystified.

"Well, I'm Lucy and, to cut a long story short, I was once, many years ago, a children's toy, a magnetic ladybird which a doctor goblin like you brought to life. Apparently, during her training she'd been told to breathe life into one small and one large object. As you can guess, I was the small one. She also said that the large object was a forklift truck, would you believe!"

"Guy Fork!!" Ten Ends couldn't believe what he was hearing. "I've met him. He was exceedingly kind, but we never said goodbye." And Ten Ends proceeded to recount his recent adventures. Lucy Ladybird listened with incredulity, but it was when he mentioned that the object of his quest was to find Doctor Loca Potion that Lucy suddenly interrupted.

"But she's the very goblin who brought me to life. She still lives in the forest, although she's now quite old. Nevertheless, she is still the Principal Doctor Goblin in this region. I can help you find her if you wish."

"Could you? Yes! Yes please! Will you take me there?" Ten Ends couldn't believe his luck. *"Or was this just luck?"* he wondered.

"I cannot leave the Compass Tree, I'm afraid. Other travellers may need help. But I can lend you my spots. They'll point you in the right direction."

Although originally a toy, and to amuse you, the young reader who delights in long words, Lady Lucy was a replica Coccinella Septempunctata, or, in English and Animal

Tongue, a red seven-spotted ladybird, and it was these spots which suddenly popped off her back, onto the ground, and formed an arrowhead.

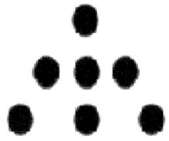

"There you are, young Ten Ends, follow my spots, wherever they lead, until you reach your destination, then please send them back to me. Be cautious, however, for the forest can be very dangerous at night. You never know who or what you might meet. Good luck!" With that, Lucy flew up into the branches of the Compass Oak, once again singing her signature song:

> ♪ *Sweetest song you ever heard,*
> *Lady Lucy, ladybird,*
> *Underneath the Compass Tree.*
> *Which direction? Just ask me!*
> *Sweetest song you ever heard,*
> *Lovely Lucy, ladybird.* ♪

All the while, Ten Ends was setting off on the next stage of his quest, with the seven-spot arrowhead pointing in the direction he was to travel. As he trudged his way, hour by hour, through the winding forest paths, with his eyes glued to the speckled marker blazing his trail, he began to wonder what lay in store for him. While his eyes had quickly grown accustomed to the leafy darkness, his mind's eye was painting a much hazier picture. Would he even find Loca? What was she like? Could she actually be

Locum's mother? How would she receive him? Would she frown at some of his less worthy escapades? Most of all, how would he ever get back to Tanglewood? He so wanted to go home again.

With dawn just a couple of hours away, Ten Ends came across a low, rotting oak stump and decided to sit down for a rest before undertaking the final stretch of his journey. He called to the seven spots who immediately understood his intentions and formed a circle on the peaty forest floor beneath his feet. He had been picking the odd bud and berry to satisfy his hunger, but his empty, rumbling stomach was clearly telling him to eat a substantial meal. With his thoughts fixed firmly on food, his short break was suddenly disturbed by the sound of someone weeping, except that it wasn't someone ... it was Poor Polly.

Poor Polly was an oak bracket, a rare fungus or polypore which grows mainly at the base of ancient oak trees. The thick amber liquid she secreted made it seem as though she were weeping honey.

"Thank goodness you've sat down here," she sobbed. "I'm so lonely, it makes me cry. It's lovely to have someone to talk to. Please stay awhile."

Ten Ends, a bit of a loner himself, immediately felt sorry for this strange, melancholy creature. "Of course, just a few minutes though. I must reach the north of the forest before daybreak. I'm Ten Ends, by the way ..."

He proceeded to tell Poor Polly all about his recent travels, while she, in turn, lamented her own sad existence.

"That's why I shed these tears of honey, you see. Are you hungry?"

As soon as she had spoken those three enticing words, the seven spots started to dart about madly, finally reforming into an arrowhead, and rushing away from the tree stump as fast as they could go. When they saw that Ten Ends hadn't followed them, they dashed back towards him and tried again.

Ten Ends, oblivious to the call of his guides, was offered a bite of fungus. "Don't worry!" Polly's tearful face broke into a smile. "It grows on me again in no time and it's delicious with a drink of my honey."

Despite his misgivings, the prospect of an appetising meal was just too much. Ten Ends loved mushrooms and liquid honey happened to be his favourite tipple. Ignoring the frantic gestures of the seven spots, he gave into temptation and reached out to Poor Polly. In a weird, rippling movement she appeared to grow a tough, rubbery arm which she bent at the elbow before breaking off a large piece of her own pungent, fibrous flesh. She handed it to Ten Ends. At the same time, she flexed her back into a channel from which her amber sap poured, filling a small hollow in the tree stump. After several bites of the fungus, Ten Ends dropped to his knees and lapped up the nectar as a cat drinks from a saucer of milk. On seeing this, Lady Lucy Ladybird's seven spots suddenly disappeared.

It wasn't long before Ten Ends began to feel the world caving in around him. His stomach ached, his head was spinning, and his legs began to crumple underneath him. As he lost consciousness, Polly used her contorting arm to pull him towards her. "Now, you stupid creature. In an hour you'll be dead meat and …" she licked her lips, "A rare treat, my mouth-watering breakfast."

As his frail body began to shut down and paralysis gradually enveloped his limbs, Ten Ends became vividly aware of his life flashing by him, the characters and events from his past.

He saw his secluded woodland home in Tanglewood where Wye's Owl kept order and dispensed justice. He squirmed at the dark days when his jealousy of Locum had flared into hatred, pain and punishment; later the period of redemption with dear Roxy Rat and her lovable ratlets. He smiled as he remembered the little spider, Cedric, and his two colourful toothbrush friends who Locum had brought to life, albeit after yet another argument he had had with his doctor goblin neighbour.

He remembered a ride on a snowman and a life and death struggle with the evil snow witch, Ebba Thrubb, when he had saved Locum from certain death. Even more vivid memories from recent times; Handsome, the lawnmower; the friendly dogs, Stan and Molly; a ride in an aeroplane and a giant bear calling himself Sir Bagworth Brown; Ducky the peregrine falcon whose name made him chuckle; Guy, the friendly forklift truck; the horrible crows, Clawdette and Clawed; helpful rabbits, Dug, Duchess and Mike; Squirm, the hospitable giant worm and lovely Lady Lucy Ladybird with her seven spots. Then, as the memories began to recede, he vaguely recalled eating a meal of mushrooms and honey while being watched by the sneering face of a … a … fungus??

With his life slowly ebbing away, a new sensation suddenly replaced his fading reminiscences. He was slumped across the back of a huge beast pounding its way through the forest paths at great speed, cajoled along by the soft but imposing voice of its mistress. When the helter-skelter journey ended, he was lifted off and placed on a soft bed of feathers and down. Had he finally gone to meet Cobalus the life-giver, he wondered? Then he felt the sharp prick of a thorn being inserted in his arm, and a liquid potion poured down his throat through a reed tube.

"Come back to us, young goblin, come back and open your eyes." It was the same voice he had heard while riding on the beast, but this time with a semblance of compassion and reassurance.

Slowly, slowly, Ten Ends opened his eyes. He was unable to speak, unable to move, but he looked up to see a very old, wiry doctor goblin grinning at him.

"I hope you enjoyed your ride on Scruffy, my wild boar. I certainly did. Quite exhilarating! I haven't travelled at that speed for years. Lucy's spots, they saved your life by the way, said that you were looking for me. Well, here I am. I'm Loca … Loca Potion!"

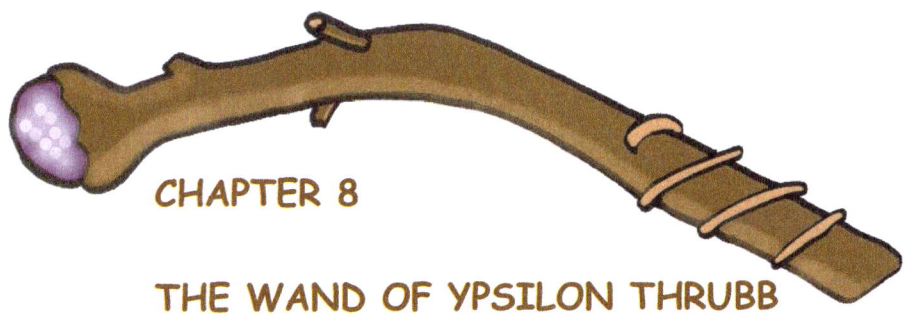

CHAPTER 8

THE WAND OF YPSILON THRUBB

"I shall soon be asking each of you five Apprentice Doctor Goblins to make the most important decision of your life, but first you must fully understand why."

Summoned to the centre of the ancient stone circle at Stonehenge, Elfric, Locum, McBrownie, Rysbottom and Tomos listened intently to the voice of Cobalus as he prepared them for the final trial in their training as Principal Doctor Goblins.

"We are goblins. Along with elves, fairies, gnomes and imps, humans choose to call us mythological creatures, or figures from folklore. What do they know! We belong to a unique mystical realm, neither human nor animal, but we share with them a seemingly unending tension between the forces of good and evil.

If we place ourselves at one end of that spectrum, then Ypsilon Thrubb and her like are most certainly at the other. The daily activities of all living creatures are delicately balanced between the two. When the spirit of darkness overshadows the world, we experience selfishness, hatred, strife, even warfare. I, Cobalus, The Shadow, entreat you, instead, to follow the virtuous path of goodness and thus bring harmony, peace, kindness and love back to our cherished realm.

But NEVER underestimate the strength of your opponent. Ypsilon Thrubb wields remarkable powers, certainly greater than your own, and she will not give up her wand lightly. If, by careful preparation, intelligence, stealth and courage, you succeed in bringing it back to Stonehenge, you will tip the balance for a whole year in favour of goodness as it will take the witch at least nine months to fashion a new wand and to teach it her malicious spells. If you all fail, however, her dark powers will prevail, and we can expect a dreadful year of turbulence.

But, be warned, this mission is extremely dangerous. It has in the past created a number of brave young martyrs, who have given their lives in the fight against evil.

As I said, it's now time to make your decision. Are you prepared and willing to undertake this trial? Nobody will think the less of you for turning away at this stage and therefore I ask, in all solemnity … are you ready to lay down your life for our beloved goblin realm?"

The apprentices looked round at each other nodding their heads in harmony, stood up, and as one shouted emphatically, "Yes! We are!"

Also in attendance at this midnight gathering were the three Cobalus Professors and Cobalt, the ghost eagle. Lusor, the senior professor, stood up to speak, and instructed the apprentices to prepare themselves for the trial.

"You will be taken west to the Great Oak Forest of Dean by Cobalt tomorrow evening at dusk. You will be given provisions which will last no more than two days, after which you must fend for yourselves. You must return by the seventh night, whether or not you are successful. We shall assume that if you have not returned by that time, you will not be returning at all!

Spend your remaining time in Grovely Wood wisely. We, the Cobalus Professors will be there to advise you. We possess maps of the Great Oak Forest, and our knowledge banks are full of facts about its plant life and inhabitants. This includes what little we have gleaned about the life and behaviour of Ypsilon Thrubb herself. Acquaint yourselves thoroughly with this precious information; it may save your life!

Now, ghost eagles, please take us back to Grovely."

Locum and Tomos spent the rest of the night and most of the following day in Grovely Wood library, ploughing through an archive of papers made available to them by the Cobalus Professors.

Elfric, McBrownie and Rysbottom, however, decided to conserve their energy for the days ahead, sleeping through the night and only returning to their studies by mid-morning the following day. They argued that, as they were the first three to be sent into the Great Oak Forest, they would need their sleep more than the other two, whom they thought of as swots rather than goblins of action.

At last, the moment arrived. It was dusk. Cobalt and the ghost eagles flew down into Grovely Wood to pick up the five apprentices along with Professor Lusor, who would supervise the timed start from a prominent twisted oak tree on the perimeter of the Great Forest. The twisted oak would be manned for the next seven nights by one of the Cobalus Professors, taking turns on watch with Cobalt until the apprentices returned.

At midnight, in an atmosphere fraught with tension and nervous excitement, the apprentice McBrownie from the Principality of Caledonia set off resolutely and with a degree of confidence on his quest to confront Ypsilon Thrubb. As the first to leave, he felt that he had a better chance than the other four apprentices. He not only possessed the element of surprise, but also, should he manage to seize the wand, he would deprive the others of the opportunity to do so themselves.

Elfric of Mercia and Rysbottom of The Ridings followed McBrownie into the forest at one-hour intervals, while Locum and Tomos passed the intervening time with their heads together in deep conversation. When his turn came, Locum acknowledged Tomos with a discreet nod of the forehead and set off alone into the forest. After walking for just five minutes, at the first fork in the path, he stopped, sat down with his legs crossed, and closed his tired eyes.

Almost exactly one hour later, by mutual agreement, he was joined by his friend Tomos who also stopped and rested. Both apprentices had decided to take a catnap before resuming their journey into the heart of the forest. The other three apprentices were already ahead of them. Locum and Tomos both agreed that their careful planning and working as a pair would give them an advantage when they confronted the witch, even though one of the other three might in the meantime be able to snatch the wand.

"I've already had a break, Tomos, so I'll search around for a trail. Let me know when you're ready to move." Locum waved and set off for a quick recce of the surrounding area. Within an hour he had returned, and the two friends departed together on their chosen path north-westwards through the Great Forest.

*****

The following night, McBrownie, the first apprentice to set off, had progressed well and was approaching the heart of the forest, although he had no idea where he was, or if Ypsilon Thrubb was anywhere nearby. He had heard that she tended to find strangers before they could find her. This being the case, he decided to draw attention to himself. From his rucksack he pulled out a set of Caledonian gnome pipes and began to play a merry tune. His plan was to play the part of the wandering minstrel. He would entertain the witch, lull her into a false sense of security, show her the pipes, let her have a try if she wished, then, while she was thus distracted, he would snatch her wand, leaving her powerless, and make his escape.

McBrownie the piper very quickly began to acquire an audience. It seemed that every forest dweller in the vicinity had gathered round in a clearing to listen to this impromptu concert. McBrownie smiled at the applause he received. Rabbits hopped, moles clapped their hands, nightingales tweeted his tunes and owls hooted. But his playing also attracted some rather less desirable characters. A fox barked a mocking laugh, two adders hissed at the piper, a group of pixies and a visiting leprechaun from the Emerald Isle sniggered derisively. Just at that moment the wasps appeared.

They flew in from the west, where the River Wye splits the forest in two. At least a thousand in number, they were led by a giant queen, weasel-sized, her yellow stripes flashing in the darkness. They hovered over McBrownie for a while, listening and weighing up the situation until eventually the queen sent a small squadron back west for further instructions. When they returned, they buzzed around the queen who immediately flew down onto a low tree branch, staring at the bewildered doctor goblin, who immediately dropped his gnome pipes. The crowd fell silent, though the more cautious managed to slip away in the darkness fearing the worst.

"Zzzzilence!" the queen spoke in a mixture of animal tongue and a high-pitched buzz. My mistrezz Ypzzilon is dizzpleased. Goblinzz are not welcome here. Dizzperzze, all of you. Zzoldier wazzps, ATTACK."

On her command, the wasps swarmed all over poor McBrownie, their poisonous stings penetrating his skin like daggers, while the rest of the spectators fled in case the wasps decided to turn on them. When his assailants finally flew away, he was left alone on the forest floor unconscious, but all the while enduring a nightmare in which his flesh burned with an agonising pain.

The first creatures to reappear on the scene were a small family of rabbits who looked around warily to make sure the coast was clear. They started to dig purposefully in the undergrowth to uproot some wild garlic bulbs, which, without delay, they began to chew. Approaching McBrownie with watchful caution, they applied the crushed, moist garlic and spittle to his stinging wounds to alleviate the pain. When they had done all they could, they dragged him back towards the safe haven of their warren but were suddenly startled by a voice from a nearby bush.

"I'll take care of him from here on but thank you for your kindness and bravery."

The terrified rabbits turned to face another doctor goblin.

"Don't be afraid. I'm his friend. I heard the pipe music but arrived too late to help him. My name is Elfric. I can take him back to a place of safety."

The matronly rabbit introduced herself as Sara. "Well Elfric, he is still unconscious and cannot be moved for at least three nights. He has had a massive dose of wasp poison. We have treated his skin to take away the pain, but even when he wakes up, he will be too weak to travel."

"Point taken, Sara. This antidote may help though." Elfric handed her a small bottle of medicine from his rucksack. "I am a doctor goblin after all!"

Elfric was now in a quandary. Should he continue with his own mission and leave McBrownie in the care of these kindly rabbits, or should he stay and help his friend to recover, after which he could assist him back to the safety of the twisted oak tree where the Cobalus Professors would be waiting. Yet he knew in his heart that McBrownie was in too bad a state to travel alone and therefore realised that both of their quests for the wand were over.

*****

Rysbottom of the Ridings arrived in the heart of the forest too late to become involved in the wasp incident which had marked the end of McBrownie and Elfric's quest for the wand. He had walked for three nights on a more westerly route through the forest than the other two. His detailed research into Ypsilon Thrubb had revealed that most sightings of her had occurred in the west and, in particular, at a place called Rat Rock overlooking the great River Wye. His maps and compass had led him there more or less without incident, apart from a brush with a rather grumpy toad called Norman who spat at Rysbottom claiming that the doctor goblin had trod on his toe. Peace was restored once Rysbottom had apologised and dug up a couple of worms for Norman's dinner.

"Here you are, Mister Toad, some supper for you." Seizing upon this opportunity, he continued, "This may seem a strange, even daring question, but do you, perchance, have any information on the whereabouts of the witch, Ypsilon Thrubb."

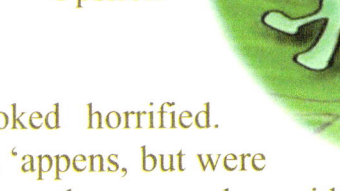

Norman looked horrified. "Oi do, as it 'appens, but were Oi you," his words were spoken with a quaint, west country drawl, "Oi'd turn around and go back the way you came! She's not one you want to meddle with. Oi've 'eard that she has a particular aversion to doctor goblins. Now why do you want to know, for Cobalus' sake?"

Rysbottom explained the purpose of his mission, putting his trust in this rather tetchy old amphibian.

"Well, Oi'd take my 'at off to you if only Oi wore one." Norman's voice had dropped to a whisper. "Everyone in the forest is frightened of 'er and it would be good if she could be taken down a peg or three. Now come with me into this old rabbit burrow where we can talk in private. She'd kill me if she found out that Oi'd helped you." He paused for a second, "… and Oi mean it, she'd kill me."

In the privacy of the burrow, Norman told Rysbottom everything he knew about Ypsilon Thrubb, the approximate whereabouts of her coven, her habits, her defences and her armoury.

"She uses an army of wasps, led by a vicious queen who does her bidding. They act as guards, watchmen and soldiers, and can inflict terrible wounds with their stings.

She also provides blackfly honeydew for giant wood ants, encouraging them to build their huge nest mounds around her covenstead in return for poisonous acid which they secrete from their stings. She uses this to dispose of her enemies, a slow and agonising death. And then, of course, there's her wand: spells, lightning bolts, the lot, though without it, she's defenceless apart, of course, from her wasps, ants and Percy and Porky."

"Percy and Porky?" Rysbottom asked enquiringly.

"Her two vicious, overweight wild boars, with only half a brain cell between them! They're the sort that attacks first and asks questions afterwards. You'll need a fair wind and lots of luck to get the better of Ypsilon Thrubb. I wish you well, brave fellow."

Rysbottom thanked Norman for his help and within minutes was on his way to Rat Rock, with his mind spinning with ideas about how he might overcome these treacherous obstacles and procure the wand.

*****

All the while, Locum and Tomos had been travelling together westwards for two nights after their careful, preparatory research had also pointed towards Rat Rock as a likely location for the witch. They had all the time been looking out for signs of the other apprentices, but without success. From the start they had planned to work together to steal the wand. Locum wanted to let Tomos take the credit for this as he was aware that his friend had scored higher in the earlier tests, and that he himself had failed to complete the first of the two trials, albeit in choosing to save the life of a small human child.

The first sign that they were nearing their quarry was the emergence of scurrying wood ants. To follow their trail might well lead them to the witch's coven, although neither Locum nor Tomos knew whether the ants would, or even could warn Ypsilon Thrubb about the presence of two doctor goblins in the vicinity. Nevertheless, they decided to follow the ants discreetly, creeping silently from tree to tree when, after just a few yards, they came across a horrifying sight. There, on the path in front of them, with ants crawling all over his body, lay Rysbottom.

CHAPTER 9

MOLLY

Molly, the brown and white spaniel Ten Ends had befriended at Heathrow Airport, was beginning to wonder whether her escape to freedom had been worthwhile. Although her owners had been strict and uncaring, at least their house in Dorset was warm and there was usually, if not always, enough food. However, she had never wanted to go with them to Spain.

After hiding among the bushes on the airport perimeter for a day or so, scavenging for scraps of human waste from the refuse bins, she decided she must leave Heathrow to explore the wider area and try to find a better place to live. As she pondered over her next steps, she began to recall the words of the friendly little doctor goblin whom she had sheltered inside her cage on the aeroplane. Ten Ends - yes, that was his name - said that late at night, near the Air Animal warehouse, he had met a very kind, talking forklift truck called Guy Fork who intimated that he might be able to help the little goblin get back to Tanglewood Deep. Ten Ends had spoken fondly of his cosy little home there, hidden under a fern-covered hump by a large beech tree. Molly made up her mind to go to Tanglewood Deep and find a new home for herself. But first, at midnight, she must pay this Guy Fork a visit.

*****

"Yes, I remember Ten Ends. Cheerful little chap with quite a tale to tell. Unfortunately, I never saw him again. We had arranged for him to meet me at midnight, but Ducky, the airport falcon who had left him in a place of safety during the day, found him gone when she went to pick him up and bring him here to me. We've since been in contact with his friends in Tanglewood via Tawny Telegraph. Although he did have an idea about first going to Savernake Forest to find Loca Potion, he always said he wanted most of all to get back home to East Anglia. I suggest you make your way there, Molly. They seem to be a friendly lot. I'm sure he'll turn up eventually."

Molly had already taken a liking to Guy and decided to put her trust in him. "Mr Fork, may I ask two favours of you, please?"

"Of course, my dear. Fire away!"

"Well, first of all, may I sleep in your cab for the night? I'm so tired of dashing from one hiding place to another at this hectic airport."

"No problem at all, Molly. Hop in! Now, what was your second question?"

"Do you think you could take me to Tanglewood?"

MOLLY

*****

Ten Ends was making good progress after his near-death experience in Savernake Forest. The effects of the poison administered to him by Poor Polly, the oak bracket fungus, were beginning to wear off. He wasn't yet strong enough to stand or walk, but his senses were returning, and he felt that he was ready, at last, to speak to Loca.

"So, what were you looking for, young fellow? Why did you want to see me in particular? Loca's voice was soft and clear, despite her great age.

Ten Ends hesitated. He was still weak, and he wasn't sure where to begin.

"Take your time, dear. There's no hurry."

"My ... my name is Ten Ends and I'm just an ordinary doctor goblin from Tanglewood in East Anglia, but I can be very stupid and thoughtless at times."

"Well, we all have our faults," Loca sighed reassuringly.

And Ten Ends began to relate the sequence of events that had brought him to Heathrow Airport. "It was there that I met Guy Fork and told him what I'm telling you now. When he heard that I had caused damage in Wicksham Parva with Handsome the lawnmower by using Cobalus irresponsibly, Guy commented that we should always have the best of intentions when using its power. To which I replied that Locum, my friend and distant cousin in Tanglewood, always used to say the very same words of caution about using Cobalus. At that point Guy nearly blew a gasket and said that Loca, who had brought him to life, had a son called Locum who had gone missing when he was just a boy."

Loca gasped. She was shocked into silence but her whole demeanour intimated that she wanted Ten Ends to continue.

"I've known Locum all my life and I always looked up to him. He never let me down, even when, in my jealousy, I nearly killed him. He always saw the good in me. I learned from him, and he encouraged me to be a better goblin, even though I still have my mischievous moments. It was one of these that caused me to run away. It was when I found myself stuck on top of a tower at Heathrow Airport that I finally came to my senses and decided to find you and tell you about Locum. I thought that it might make amends for all my misdeeds. So here I am."

Their conversation continued throughout the night. Loca said that she had always known that Cobalus, The Shadow, wanted to train Locum. "He was such a bright boy, you know." Unlike the other residents of Savernake, she realised straightaway that it was Cobalt, the ghost eagle, who had snatched him from her. After that, she never knew where he had gone, or even if he was still alive. Perhaps he had been killed on one of his apprenticeship trials?

This aspect of doctor goblin life was a revelation to Ten Ends. He realised that he wasn't well-behaved or smart enough to become a Principal Doctor Goblin, one of the Chosen Few, but Locum? Locum, who had been far too modest to tell him that he himself was one? He was just his neighbour, friend and distant cousin although he had never asked about his past or found out whether they were actually related.

Once again Ten Ends startled Loca, albeit with his next question.

"Doctor Loca, will you travel with me back to Tanglewood? I'm not good with directions and we could confirm once and for all whether or not Locum is your son."

"Well, Ten Ends. You have certainly taken my breath away and stirred up feelings inside that I thought were buried in the past. My life would most certainly be complete if I were able to see my son again. However, it will be difficult for me to leave here. I am old and although I am still active, I'm not sure that I'd be strong enough to take on such a long journey. And, of course, I still have my duties as Principal Doctor Goblin and many patients to see, let alone treating young doctor goblins who have been poisoned by a fungus! Nevertheless, when you have fully recovered, I shall help you to return to Tanglewood. We have many friends we can call on to provide transport and show you the way."

The next few days saw Ten Ends grow stronger and stronger, while Loca was able to call on the services of the Tawny Telegraph who, as well as hooting a chain of messages to each other, were also able to transport small loads for long distances along this chain.

When the night came for Ten Ends to leave Savernake Forest, Loca handed him a letter for her son, bearing a message of love and hope that they could, after so many years, meet together again.

As Ten Ends flew off on the back of Lily, a beautiful tawny owl, he turned his head and saw Loca beneath him, waving, with tears in her eyes. But when he looked again, he fancied that he saw a huge golden bird lifting her up to the sky and carrying her away to the south.

*****

MOLLY

Well before dawn at Heathrow Airport, Guy Fork woke his little guest with a brief cough from his starter motor.

"Wake up, Molly, I've something to tell you and someone I'd like you to meet."

Molly stood up slowly, stretching her legs out in front and shaking her floppy ears.

"Oh, good morning Guy. I've had a lovely night's sleep. Thank you for your hospitality."

"Well, Molly, I shall be driven to work soon and will have to say goodbye before my driver arrives. Now come down here; I want you to meet my friend Prendergast."

Guy opened his cab door allowing Molly to jump down on to the concourse. At the same time a sleek, grey pigeon flew down from his cab roof.

"Molly, this is Prendergast, one of the country's network of missing homing pigeons."

"Good morning, Molly!"

"Nice to meet you, Prendergast! Homing pigeons? Missing?"

Guy explained. "I cannot take you home, Molly. I'm needed at the airport.

Besides, there is no way I could drive along the main human roads with a dog in the driving seat! I think we might be noticed, even at night. This is where Prendergast comes in.

Human pigeon fanciers keep birds like Prendergast in cages in their back yards. On competition days they are driven hundreds of miles to a starting point where they are released, along with homing pigeons belonging to other owners from the same club. The humans have prizes and trophies for the first pigeon to return home to its cage.

Now while most pigeons put up with this life, they are, after all, well fed and looked after, there are also some who hate being stuck in a cage all day and long to be free. These are the homing pigeons who have 'gone missing', that is they have never returned to their owners. They have established a network of their own, which any animal can use to guide them when travelling long distances. After all, they have an acute sense of direction and know the country like the back of their claws."

Prendergast took up the story and told Molly his plan. "We shall leave the airport after midnight when the humans take to their beds. You will be walking with me on your back to guide you. I will take you across fields and through woods, keeping well away from human habitations. It is over a hundred miles to Tanglewood, and I reckon you can walk about twenty miles in a day. So, hide away and rest up until tonight. We have a long journey ahead of us."

*****

"Quickly Tomos! He's still breathing. We have to help him." The young apprentice Locum was kneeling over Rysbottom whose bare torso, arms and legs were covered in stings and bite marks, while his back had suffered an even graver wound, where a large blunt point had penetrated. Tomos bent down, brushing away the wood ants that covered his body, while Locum, shaking his head, tried in vain to stem the flow of blood from the wound on his back.

Rysbottom lay on his side, almost oblivious to the searing pain shooting through his body. He forced his eyes open and, seeing Locum, he murmured … "Let me be. It's no use, I'm done for. You must listen; I know how you can steal the wand. Hear me out!"

Gasping for breath and in great pain, Rysbottom told Locum and Tomos that he'd used an ancient goblin spell, the Chameleon, to get right up close to Ypsilon Thrubb.

Locum recalled the Chameleon spell. It had been widely used by goblins in times long past, when the earth was covered in forests and heaths, when humans were few and far between, before they had built towns and roads, and goblins could walk safely in daylight. On the rare occasion when a goblin saw a human, he would invoke the Chameleon spell and lie flat on the ground. His clothes, skin and hair would change colour to match the background and he'd become virtually invisible. Since those times, humans had claimed the land for themselves, building their cities and motorways, while goblins had been forced to retreat to the remaining remote woodlands and become creatures of the night.

"Neither the witch nor her guards saw me creeping flat along the rocky ground in front of her. She has a swarm of wasps buzzing around her head, massive anthills and two huge wild boars strategically placed either side of her rock hewn throne. I leapt up, snatched the wand from her hand and ran, thinking I'd be camouflaged, but as soon as I reached the grass trail, they saw me. I had no time to cast a second Chameleon spell to change colour again. The wasps attacked and I was spiked by one of the boars, as the foul witch cackled her venomous curses."

Rysbottom was fading fast but, with great strength of will, managed to utter his final instructions.

"Your best chance is from behind. The back of her throne is the highest point of Rat Rock. Behind it is a 600-foot drop to the River Wye below. While one of you creates a diversion in the forest, the other must climb the cliff, grab the wand from behind and dash back over the top.

You'll need aerial transport to escape, and your best bet is a pair of peregrine falcons … They have been forced to nest on a ledge on the cliff … after … she seized … their favourite nesting place … at the top … her throne. The rest is … up to you. I … I … did … my best!"

Rysbottom's eyes closed again, and the life spirit drained gently from him. There was a rush of air and the voice of Cobalus could be heard calling him home. Locum and Tomos watched with sorrow and awe as the brave young goblin from The Ridings disappeared within a whirlwind up into the sky.

CHAPTER 10

THE BOGEYMAN

Molly's journey to Tanglewood had, up to that point, been fairly uneventful, that is apart from one curious incident. Prendergast Pigeon, perched on her back, had guided her along country pathways and through woodland at night, avoiding human habitation wherever possible. As they grew in confidence, however, they decided to take a slight risk. They had reached the edge of a small village called Great Safford when Prendergast suggested a short cut through the main street.

"It's well past midnight. Nobody will be about, and it will save us a three-mile detour round the fields. Anyway, if we see a human, you can scamper away, and I'll fly ahead and meet you on the other side of the village."

Molly was very much in favour of shortening the journey whenever possible and nodded her consent to Prendergast's plan. But as they passed the Red Lion Inn, a few rowdy youngsters, slightly the worse for wear, fell out of the pub door and poured into the street.

"Look at that, lads," shouted a large gruff fellow going by the nickname of Gussy. "There's a sight you don't see too often, a dawg with a pigeon on its back!" Immediately one of Gussy's mates, Aaron, pulled out his mobile phone and took a photograph of this unusual sight, a photo which subsequently went 'viral'. Molly and Prendergast were, of course, blissfully unaware of their instant celebrity, for the simple and obvious reason that neither of them happened to possess a mobile phone!

The two weary travellers, wondering what all the fuss was about, made their way swiftly out of the village and continued their journey eastwards.

*****

Ten Ends, meanwhile, was enjoying, or rather enduring, a series of night rides towards Tanglewood on the back of a succession of tawny owls. Being territorial by nature, each owl carried him only to the next tawny's domain, no more than a mile away, where, by a hooted arrangement, he would be picked up again and transported to the next stage. As the journey from Savernake Forest to

Tanglewood was well over a hundred miles, Ten Ends soon lost count of the number of lifts he had taken. Like human taxi drivers, some of the tawnies were full of cheerful conversation and were curious to know everything about his journey and adventures, while others were taciturn, even resentful that they were expected to turn out on a rainy night to provide an unpaid lift to a stupid doctor goblin.

After fifty or so stages of a journey which had passed smoothly and without incident, out of the blue a tawny owl failed to turn up for a changeover, hooting to his predecessor that he had a nasty cold. Ten Ends was advised to walk the next mile to a place called Boggart Grove where another owl would be waiting to pick him up.

It made a pleasant change to stretch his legs as he sauntered alone across open farm fields in the fresh night air. Flying on the back of an owl could be quite exhilarating, but it had begun to lose its appeal over such long distances. A sleepy Ten Ends had once or twice recalled the twin dangers of dropping off, a sensation he had previously felt on the top of the control tower at Heathrow Airport! Eventually he spotted the hazy outline of a large clump of trees looming in the distance.

Boggart Grove, or Scales Grove as it was known to humans, had a rather sinister reputation in folklore.

A boggart, or bogeyman, was, in size, midway between a goblin and a human and was known for its malicious pranks and, all too often, evil deeds.

At its worst, in northern lands, boggarts had even snatched away small children and young animals for the dubious pleasure of seeing how much stress it would bring to their grieving parents.

Entering the wooded grove and expecting to see a friendly tawny owl waiting to take him on the next leg of his journey, Ten Ends was stopped in his tracks by a bald, unworldly, ape-like creature, more than twice his size, glowering down at him.

"Hello Ten Ends! I've been waiting for you. Please allow me to introduce myself. I'm Humphrey, Humphrey Boggart, your local bogeyman."

Ten Ends turned to run, but the hideous creature was standing in front of him, whichever way he faced. "Escape is out of the question, I'm afraid. You cannot outrun an apparition. You're coming with me to my underground hollow. I need you to entertain me. You can tell me all about your adventures, although I've heard a great deal already. Tawny Telegraph is an excellent information channel."

"So that's how he knew my name!" Ten Ends supposed.

"Prepare yourself for a long sojourn in my little glade. I have two friends I'd like you to meet."

"Bogeyman? Bogeyman? Where have I heard that word before?" Ten Ends silent thoughts distracted him from the imminent danger in which he found himself.

"Now shift yourself!" Humphrey grabbed Ten Ends' arm and dragged him along a dark, overgrown path to the centre of the woodland grove.

"Bogeyman … a song … my grandmother's song. Hush, hush … Bogeyman …" It was on the tip of his tongue, though Ten Ends kept his thoughts to himself.

"Down there!" bellowed Humphrey, "and hurry up!"

Ten Ends was bundled down a long, hollow tunnel into a spacious underground cavern, illuminated by an army of glow worms. Humphrey pushed him across the floor towards a door, which he unlocked with a large key.

"I shall speak with you after I've had a sleep and eaten my breakfast. Now, say hello to your fellow inmates, Molly and Prendergast!"

*****

"Right, Tomos, we must make plans." Locum addressed his fellow apprentice with tears still moistening his eyes. "Poor Rysbottom. We must not allow his sad passing to have been in vain. He has pointed the way and we must follow."

"I'm with you Locum, my friend. But we have an important decision to make. Which of us will climb the rock and who will create the diversions?"

"I've been thinking about that. Unless it's the last resort or you decline the opportunity, Tomos, you should be the one to scale the cliff and take the wand back to Stonehenge. You are the more worthy. I was unable to complete the last trial and your marks in training have usually been higher than mine. Besides, I've spent most of my childhood in a flat forest, whereas you were brought up in the mountains of Cambria. I expect you'll be able to shin up Rat Rock like a mountain goat and I'm not sure how I'd cope looking down a cliff face!"

"You don't look down!" Tomos laughed, but he acknowledged that he loved climbing as a boy and was probably the best suited to the task. "Now, you must think of some convincing diversions in the forest, while I go and find a friendly peregrine falcon or two. Don't start until I come back with help. We must plan the raid and its timing to the last second.

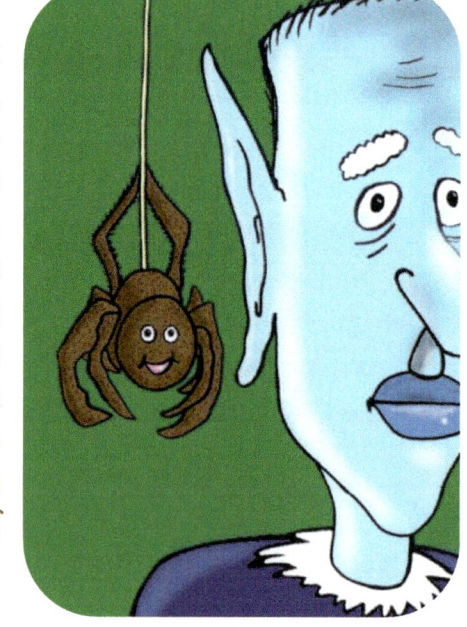

As Tomos set off to seek help for the escape flight, Locum sat down on a well-hidden, fallen log hoping to find some inspiration. Whereas Tomos' task was well defined, despite being highly dangerous, he was struggling to come up with some diversionary tactics that stood at least a reasonable chance of success.

"Need help do you?" A small spider had dropped down on Locum's shoulder.

"I overheard you two talking. I presume you're after Ypsilon's wand. The peaceful life of the forest is greatly troubled in those years when you Cobalus apprentices fail to take it from her. But all you need to do is to ask for help. It's no use being brave if you are also foolhardy and ill-prepared. I'm Cecil, by the way, and I have a wide network of friends who have as little time for Ypsilon Thrubb as you do."

"Well, Cecil, my name is Locum and you are right, we have come to seize the wand. I'd certainly welcome some assistance, but what do you suggest?"

"Why! Spiders, bees and hedgehogs of course!"

*****

"That's it! I've remembered! The Bogeyman song."

Ten Ends was sitting on the floor behind a locked door in Humphrey's underground hovel. Molly Spaniel was lying beside him with Prendergast Pigeon roosting on Molly's back, a warm soft bed. Molly could hardly believe her eyes when Ten Ends had been thrown into the room by the brutish Boggart. In spite of the awful predicament in which they found themselves, they were at the same time overjoyed to see each other and began to plan a future for Molly in Tanglewood. Ten Ends didn't want to raise her hopes too much, but he had in mind a human family which he knew would provide her with a loving home. Also, having found Loca, he now felt more confident about returning to Tanglewood Deep and facing Locum and Wye's Owl.

"What's this Bogeyman song then, Ten Ends?" Molly lifted her head and looked at the little doctor goblin with wide enquiring eyes.

"It's our way out of here!" Ten Ends was grinning with excitement. "It's called 'Hush, hush, hush, here comes the Bogeyman.' My grandmother used to sing it to us when we were children, especially if we were frightened of the dark. Anyway, one of the verses goes like this:

'Hush, hush, hush, here comes the Bogeyman,
Don't let him come too close to you,
He'll catch you if he can!

That's us, you see. But then it continues ...

Just pretend he isn't really there,
And you will find that Bogeyman will vanish in thin air.'

So, when Humphrey comes in to torment us again, we must simply do just that – pretend he isn't there and keep talking among ourselves."

"What shall we talk about?" Prendergast looked confused.

"Anything at all ... er, what you like to eat, for example."

It wasn't long before Molly twitched her nose as she sensed that Humphrey was approaching. The key turned in the lock and the Bogeyman stomped in: "Don't even think of making a break for the door. I'm quicker than all of you!"

"Did you say sunflower seed, Prendergast?"

"Be quiet all of you. I want to ask you some questions."

"Yes, it's my absolute favourite bird food, Molly. What make of dog food do you like?"

"Silence I said! What do you think you are doing?" Humphrey's voice grew louder, his tone angrier.

"Yummydog, without a doubt! Lovely meaty chunks!"

"Well, I love an autumn berry stew." It was Ten Ends' turn to chip into the conversation. By now, the Bogeyman was fuming.

"SHUT UP! STOP TALKING ABOUT FOOD, WILL YOU!!"

"The best thing about Yummydog is the gravy."

"S … S … STOP IT … S … STOP IT …", but this time Humphrey's voice was becoming shaky and his body started to take on a translucent glow.

"If I can't get hold of sunflower seed, wheat grain makes an excellent substitute."

Molly, Ten Ends and Prendergast looked around the room as a hazy cloud of light disappeared through the unlocked door, and the three friends found that they were alone.

"We've done it!" shouted Ten Ends triumphantly. "Let's get out of here. Oh, I'd forgotten. I must find the local Tawny Telegraph owl and tell him he's no longer needed. We'll all walk home together, however long it takes!" Ten Ends and Prendergast jumped on Molly's back. "Lead the way, Prendergast! We're off to Tanglewood Deep!"

*****

Locum was in deep discussion with Cecil the Spider when Tomos flew in on the back of a beautiful, blue and white peregrine falcon, whom he introduced as Renée.

"I had to climb halfway up Rat Rock to get to her nest. I'm exhausted already." Tomos winked at Locum with a mischievous grin on his face. "Renée and her mate Raoul have agreed to help us."

"Renée and Raoul? The two of you are from France?" Locum expressed genuine curiosity.

"Don't be surprised, Locum. Our parents flew here from Britanny long before we were hatched. After all, peregrine means 'foreigner'."

"Of course, no matter. Besides, we are most grateful for your assistance in our perilous venture."

"Yes, we'll do everything we can. We used to nest on the top of the rock until Ypsilon Thrubb turned up with her vicious entourage; the wasps, the wood ants and those bully-boy boars. It would be a bonus if we could drive her and her kind out of the forest for good."

"Let's see if we can take the wand first. That'll weaken her defences after which, who knows what! Locum, how have you got on?" Tomos hadn't noticed the little spider sitting on Locum's shoulder.

"Cecil here has arranged everything. Our two armies and ten leaf buckets full of honey will be arriving at any moment!"

And so the carefully planned assault on Ypsilon Thrubb's cliff top citadel began. Tomos and Cecil led a huge army of spiders through the forest to the point where the cliff plunged down to the River Wye below, though some distance from the high peak at Rat Rock where the enemy was based. They scrambled vertically downwards some twenty feet or so, then circled round to a point immediately below and behind the witch's throne where they waited in silence. Renée and Raoul returned to their nest beneath, poised and ready for their rescue mission.

At the same time, Locum and Horace, a general in command of some 50 hedgehogs, approached the citadel in silence from the front, where Ypsilon's forces were concentrated. Although the forest offered some cover, the witch's armies of wasps and ants patrolled the area regularly, so they stayed down wind of these vicious creatures and advanced slowly and stealthily. Locum crept along ahead, going as near as he could to the enemy camp before stopping. As Rysbottom had suggested, he found a small area of mossy ground just a few yards from the bare rock of the citadel and, flattening himself on the ground, he invoked the Chameleon spell. In his hand he was holding a reed whistle.

Just at that moment, a small group of wood ants walked over him, suspiciously aware of an alien scent. Face down, Locum dragged the whistle up to his mouth and blew as hard as he could. It was the signal for some fifty hedgehogs to invade the enemy camp. They targetted the ants, a tasty meal for hedgehogs, while their tough, prickly skins were impervious to the wasp stings. Occasionally they were butted and wounded by Percy and Porky, Ypsilon Thrubb's revolting wild boars. However, by curling into a ball, they simply rolled away from danger, straightened up and resumed their attack. As a further diversion a small squad of ten hedgehogs nosed the honey buckets into the battle scene and tipped them out all over the wasp nests.

Ypsilon Thrubb herself, shrieking commands to her troops, began to use her wand to cast lightning strikes to stun the hedgehogs. But before she could stand and use her full range of powers and spells, she suddenly found herself covered by a host of spiders, spinning their webs across her whole body, arms and legs, pinning her to the throne. Even more spiders sealed the giant ant hills, preventing entry or exit to the beleaguered ants. The enemy wasp attack had also lost its sting as the honeytrap had lured the wasps away from the battle into an indulgent, gluttonous feast.

At this point, Tomos appeared over the cliff top and leapt over the back of the throne, landing on Ypsilon's lap. Running down her arm, he tried to grab the wand, but was repelled by a massive electric shock. He fell to the rocky floor where he was immediately attacked by Percy the boar, who badly gashed his legs. He struggled to his feet, but the boar came at him again, but this time, it swung away at the last moment. Hanging on to Percy's tail was Locum.

"Use the power of Cobalus, Locum!" The young apprentice sensed rather than heard the Voice speaking to him. Immediately he felt that he was in control. The boar was his to command. Using its tail as a joystick he found he could both change direction and vary its speed. Moving towards the forest to gain maximum impetus, he swung back round and headed straight for the throne.

The impact was decisive. Ypsilon Thrubb, imprisoned by a giant spiders' web, and thus unable to avoid the charging boar, gasped in agony as it thudded into her stomach. Winded and screaming, she dropped her wand.

"Grab the wand Tomos! I'll get us out of here." Locum released Percy, who, in a confusion of loyalties, thundered away and launched an attack on his former partner, Porky. Locum, meanwhile, had rushed over to Tomos and hauled him from the ground. Without delay, the gallant pair headed for the cliff edge with Locum shouting to the hedgehogs and spiders, urging them to retreat, but they seemed to be enjoying the fray and, in particular, making life uncomfortable for the much-despised witch. Perhaps she would leave the Great Forest forever.

With Tomos clinging firmly to the wand with his left hand and his right arm wrapped round Locum's shoulder for support, they peered down the cliff face where Renée and Raoul were waiting to catch them. "Jump!" shouted Locum, and the two doctor goblins, covered in bruises and wasp stings, leapt triumphantly over the cliff top.

CHAPTER 11

THE POND OF REFLECTION

The man in the moon sent a beaming smile through the treetops where Locum and Ten Ends were sitting in quiet reflection, sipping a cup of honey mead in armchairs set beside the shimmering pond at the heart of Tanglewood Deep. Ten Ends' remorseful return coupled with the widespread news of his daring mission to discover Loca, had established a new relationship between the two doctor goblins. Locum was seeing a new side to his once wayward neighbour and had begun to recognise a growing maturity in him. They were becoming good friends. What's more, as each goblin unlocked memory's door to the other, their recollections were mirrored in the still waters of the pond, with vivid images of the characters they had met reflecting back for both to see.

Ten Ends spoke openly and truthfully about his journey, reckless decisions, false friends, unforeseen dangers, but most of all about the good, kind creatures he had met; Stanley, the Sorting Office labrador, Sir Bagworth Brown, the great bear who had helped the animals to escape from the plane; (Locum had looked slightly sceptical as Ten Ends recounted that little escapade); Dug, Duchess and Mike, the rabbits who had helped him make the journey to Savernake Forest; Squirm the Worm who had given him shelter; Lady Lucy Ladybird who had loaned him her spots to guide him; Prendergast Pigeon who was, no doubt, now showing another weary traveller the way home.

In particular, he remembered Guy Fork and Ducky. They had tried their best to protect and advise him, but he had unwisely chosen to throw his lot in with the false-hearted Clawdette Crow and he had left them wondering what had become of him. Since his return, however, he had sent them both messages of explanation and grateful thanks through Tawny Telegraph.

And, of course, there was Molly. They had become good friends on the aeroplane to Spain but had grown even closer on the walk back to Tanglewood. Ten Ends had been in touch with Cedric the Spider since his return. Bertie and Belinda, the Cobalus toothbrushes who lived under the same roof as Cedric, had spoken in secret to their human children, Millie and Bobby, who, in turn, had managed to persuade their parents, Mr and Mrs Evershed, to adopt this lovely brown and white spaniel. Despite some misgivings, the Eversheds advertised to see if anyone claimed this stray with no collar tag, and, since there had been no response, they had gladly taken her in, much to everyone's delight. She was showered with love and fuss. Molly had never been happier. She had found her forever home.

"Locum," Ten Ends approached the subject delicately, "I hope you don't mind me asking, but what happened to you after the ghost eagle had taken you from Savernake Forest when you were just a young boy?" This much Ten Ends already knew from the time he had spent recuperating in the forest with Loca.

Locum pondered and took another sip of mead. He trusted Ten Ends. It was time to tell his tale.

"It began with a great golden bird, a ghost eagle called Cobalt, some forty years ago. I was just ten, on my way home from school …

*****

… and so we jumped off Rat Rock where, with magnificent aerial acrobatics, we were plucked from the sky by Renée and Raoul, the peregrine falcons from France. They flew us back to the other side of the Great Forest, where the Cobalus Professors, Cobalt the ghost eagle and the other apprentices, Elfric and McBrownie, were all waiting.

McBrownie had received excellent medical attention and had recovered sufficiently from his wounds to be flown back to Stonehenge with the rest of us. At a formal gathering in the stone circle, Tomos handed the wand over to Lusor, the senior Cobalus Professor, who ceremoniously broke it in two before the voice of Cobalus addressed us.

The Shadow paid homage first of all to Rysbottom, whose bravery had shown us the way to capture the wand. As he did so, we saw Rysbottom's face smiling at us through the archway of the great Trilithon.

The Shadow then confirmed that our apprenticeships were completed. Lusor presented us with our certificates. Tomos and I were conferred as Principal Doctor Goblins,

Elfric and McBrownie as Assistant Principals. There were vacancies in two Principalities. Tomos was sent to take charge in the mountains of Cambria, where he had lived as a child. Cobalt flew me to Tanglewood, although, at my request, he called in at Shaston on the way.

I was thus able to thank the foxes, Luey and Sammie, who had provided me with food and shelter for the night on my first trial there. Local animal gossip, however, had informed them of a rumour that I had been turned into a garden gnome, a rumour which my visit immediately dispelled.

So finally I came here as the Principal Doctor Goblin of Anglia, where I have remained for nearly thirty years."

Ten Ends had hung on Locum's every word. "Wow! What a story! But there's one thing I've always wanted to ask you, Locum. Although I have all too often let you down, I have always looked up to you as a kind of wise uncle or older cousin, but are we actually related?"

"I was there at your birth, Ten Ends, as your local doctor. You were always told that I was a distant cousin, but we are not really blood relations. It's just that I was like an uncle to you after your father died, when you were still just a baby. I kept a paternal eye on you to help your mother out. Poor woman! She was rushed off her feet bringing up the ten of you."

Their conversation was suddenly interrupted by the reflection of Wye's Owl flying in across the pond.

"I'm glad I've found you two," he hooted from a perch on a nearby tree branch. "I have just received an urgent Tawny Telegram from Stonehenge. Isn't that the sacred gathering place for you doctor goblins? Anyway, it decreed, decreed, mind you, that you should both be ready to receive important visitors to-whit tomorrow, one hour after midnight. You are to-whit to meet in the clearing beneath the Great Oak, my home. Just the two of you, fair warning! Lusor, that was the sender's name, sounded very old and very important according to the first Tawny messenger. I wouldn't be late if I were you."

Wye's Owl flew off abruptly, as if to emphasise the importance of the message. Locum and Ten Ends sat staring at each other, amazed and bewildered.

*****

Not long after midnight the following evening, Locum and Ten Ends made their way along a well-worn path to the glade where stood the Great Oak tree, Wye's Owl's stately home. An eerie silence pervaded the night air and Locum sensed an atmosphere of tense expectation. He imagined that a thousand eyes were watching him. He couldn't believe that not one single small, prying creature had overheard Wye's Owl passing on the telegram message the previous evening; a spider, a small bird, a mouse or perhaps even a mole, Tanglewood gossip spread very quickly. Surely the woodland creatures already knew about the high-level visit, so why were they not all rushing to the glade to grab a front row seat?

Wye's Owl was the reason. Under threat from Tanglewood's most senior and respected law enforcement officer, the woodland creatures had stayed away. Ten Ends remembered only too well a 100-day community service sentence served on him by Wye's Owl for severe wrong-doing, a shameful occasion when Locum himself had been his victim. To Locum's great credit, he had kept faith in the young goblin and Ten Ends had managed to turn his life round.

Exactly one hour after midnight, with Wye's Owl looking down from his tree hollow nest and Locum and Ten Ends sitting nervously on an old mole hill, the distinguished visitors from Stonehenge arrived, regally transported by Cobalt the Ghost Eagle and three of his clones. Ten Ends recognised just one, Loca Potion, the Principal Doctor Goblin for Wessex, although he last remembered seeing her being carried away from Savernake Forest by one of these great birds.

Locum, however, recognised all four of the visitors, although he had not seen any of them for many, many years. There before him, stood Lusor, the senior Cobalus Professor who, despite his great age, seemed no older than he was when Locum last saw him. Also, with the two of them smiling cheerfully, he recognised his fellow apprentice trainees, now Assistant Principals Elfric and McBrownie.

However, on seeing Loca, he knew immediately that he was staring at his own dearly beloved mother. He leapt up from his grassy seat, rushed across the glade and threw his arms around her.

They would have time that evening to talk, but now was the moment for tears. Even Cobalt felt a droplet running down his feathered cheek.

Eventually Loca broke the silence. "Locum, my dear son, where do I find the words to express my joy! Yet we have two people to thank for this wonderful reunion. The first is my senior Cobalus Professor here, Lusor. Yes, I did say 'my'. The recent sad loss of our dear Professor Fleur had left a vacancy in Grovely Wood. I have been greatly honoured by Cobalus, The Shadow, and have been elevated to the position of Cobalus Professor myself."

Everyone present immediately burst into a round of spontaneous applause. Ten Ends, clapping loudly and enthusiastically, now understood why she had been taken from Savernake.

"And secondly," Loca continued, "is this fellow here." She pointed at Ten Ends. "Without his visit to my home in Savernake Forest, a journey that was fraught with danger and nearly cost him his life, I would have known nothing about you, my son, and your life here. It is a convention that Apprentice Doctor Goblins are completely separated from their families in order for them to focus on the training and dedication required to become one of the Chosen Few. Thank you both, Ten Ends and Cobalus Professor Lusor, for bringing me here today to be with my son Locum."

More applause from all present.

Professor Lusor was the next to speak, but now the whole mood of the gathering changed.

"While I am delighted to be here this night, to meet you all and to see mother and son reunited, Cobalus, The Shadow, has asked me to draw to your attention a particularly disturbing chain of events. I have to report the arrival of a new force of evil in Cambria, the Principality administered by a former fellow apprentice, your friend, Principal Doctor Goblin Tomos." Ten Ends realised that Lusor was specifically addressing Locum, Elfric and McBrownie. "I have been asked to send Tomos urgently needed assistance. This is why I have come here tonight. Locum and Elfric will travel to the mountains of Cambria tomorrow. Locum has more than once demonstrated his suitability for this kind of task. Elfric, by helping the badly wounded McBrownie all those years ago, was denied the chance of completing his final trial. Now is the opportunity for you, Elfric, to show your mettle. McBrownie, you will be given oversight of the Principality of Anglia during Locum's absence, by its very nature, an indefinable period of time. We wish you good fortune in your first position as Principal Doctor Goblin.

However, with respect, while Locum, Elfric and Tomos have the knowledge and experience to deal with this malicious and ill-willed adversary, they are both, dare I say, a little less active these days than they once were! For this reason I am sending another with you, one who is not afraid of danger, who is young, quick in mind and body, bold enough to take risks and in this instance has, I know, already had a life-threatening encounter with this evil opponent. If this young goblin proves his worth, he will be sent to Stonehenge to begin his apprenticeship to become one of the Chosen Few. Ten Ends, YOU will be accompanying Locum and Elfric to Cambria!"

A mask of disbelief shrouded Ten Ends' face. He felt stunned though proud, terrified but excited, burdened by this massive responsibility, yet inspired by such a unique opportunity. He didn't know what to say but after what seemed a lifetime, he managed to splutter a few words.

"P … Professor Lusor, thank you!! Thank you!! I … I shan't let you down, I promise you. Thank you!!" Then again, as he thought more about the task ahead, "B … but am I allowed to ask one question?"

"Of course, Ten Ends. Go ahead."

"What … what is this evil force in Cambria?"

Suddenly, the full attention of all the doctor goblins and Wye's Owl too, was focussed on Cobalus Professor Lusor.

"Oh, didn't I say? My, my! Well, you may, or may not know that the evil witch, Ypsilon Thrubb, has a daughter, far more malicious, considerably more cruel and, I regret to say, immeasurably more powerful. I refer, of course, to the dastardly snow witch, Ebba Thrubb!"

THE END

ABOUT THIS BOOK

Doctor Goblins! marks a departure from the author's trilogy featuring Cedric the Spider, though the main characters, Locum and Ten Ends, first appear in those earlier tales.

The format of the book differs too. Single chapter bedtime stories are replaced by a full children's fantasy novel, interweaving the adventures of the two main characters and featuring two time periods distanced by a generation of doctor goblins.

Illustrations are, for the first time, in full colour throughout. The historical sections featuring Locum's apprenticeship are highlighted by a change in font (Times New Roman) and font colour (sepia).

The age range for readers is also a little higher, probably more suited to children of 8 years or older. As ever, there exists a subliminal text for the satirical amusement of parents and guardians.

Jack Webb is a pseudonym. The author lives in the English county of Suffolk, with the place names in the book providing many clues as to the exact whereabouts!

Printed in Great Britain
by Amazon